Agatha Raisin
and the
Haunted House

The Agatha Raisin series
(listed in order)

Agatha Raisin and the Haunted House

M. C. Beaton

ROBINSON
London

Constable & Robinson Ltd
3 The Lanchesters
162 Fulham Palace Road
London W6 9ER
www.constablerobinson.com

First published in the US 2003 by St Martin's Press
175 Fifth Avenue, New York, NY 10010

First published in the UK by Robinson,
an imprint of Constable & Robinson Ltd 2006

A copy of the British Library Cataloguing in
Publication data is available from the British Library

ISBN 13: 978-1-84529-380-2
ISBN 10: 1-84529-380-0

Printed and bound in the EU

5 7 9 10 8 6 4

For Edwina Mori,
with love

Chapter One

Foot-and-mouth disease had closed down the countryside. Country walks and farm gates were padlocked. The spring was chilly and wet, with the first daffodils hanging their yellow heads under torrents of rain.

The thatch on Agatha Raisin's cottage dripped mournfully. She sat on the kitchen floor with her cats and wondered what to do to ward off a familiar feeling of approaching boredom. With boredom came nervous depression, as she well knew.

An interesting-looking man had moved into the cottage next door, formerly owned by her ex-husband, James, but interest in any man at all had died in Agatha's bosom. She had not joined the other village ladies in taking around cakes or home-made jam. Nor had she heard any of the gossip because she had just returned from London where, in her capacity as freelance public relations officer, she had been helping to launch a new fashion line for young people called Mr Harry. All it had served to do was make middle-aged Agatha feel old. Some of the skinny models – heroin-chic was still the fashion – had made her feel fatter and older. Her conscience had disturbed her because she knew the clothes were made in Taiwan out of the cheapest material and guaranteed to fall apart at the seams if worn for very long.

She got to her feet and went upstairs to her bedroom and studied herself in a full-length mirror. A stocky middle-aged woman with good legs, shiny brown hair, and small bearlike eyes stared back at her.

Action, she said to herself. She would put on make-up and go and see her friend Mrs Bloxby, the vicar's wife, and catch up on the village gossip. Agatha put on a foundation base of pale make-up, reflecting that it was not so long ago when bronzed skin had been all the rage. Now that the unfashionable could afford to go abroad in the middle of winter, it was no longer smart to sport a tan or even to wear brownish make-up. She plucked nervously at the skin under her chin. Was it getting loose? She slapped herself under the chin sixty times and then was cross to see a red flush on her neck.

She changed out of the old trousers and sweater she had put on that morning and decided on a biscuit-coloured linen suit over a gold silk blouse. Not that this sudden desire to dress up had anything to do with the new owner of the cottage next door, she told herself. At least, as the cliché went, time was a great healer. She hardly ever thought of James now and had given up any hope of seeing him again.

Back downstairs, she shrugged into her Burberry and picked up a golf umbrella and went out into the pouring rain. Why on earth had she worn high heels? she wondered, as she picked her way round the puddles on Lilac Lane and headed for the vicarage.

Mrs Bloxby, a gentle-faced woman with grey hair, opened the door of the vicarage to her. 'Mrs Raisin!' she cried. 'When did you get back?'

'Last night,' said Agatha, reflecting that after London, the formal use of her second name sounded odd. But then the village ladies' society of which Agatha was a member always addressed one another formally.

'Come in. Such dreadful weather. And this foot-and-mouth plague is frightening. Ramblers have been told not to walk the countryside, but they won't listen. I really don't think some of those ramblers even like the countryside.'

'Any foot-and-mouth around here yet?' asked Agatha, taking off her coat and hanging it on a peg in the hall.

'No, nothing round Carsely . . . yet.'

She led the way into the sitting-room and Agatha followed. Agatha sank down into the feather cushions on the old sofa, took off her shoes and stretched her wet stockinged feet out to the fire.

'I'll lend you a pair of wellingtons when you leave,' said Mrs Bloxby. 'I'll get some coffee.'

9

Agatha leaned back and closed her eyes as Mrs Bloxby went off to the kitchen. It suddenly felt good to be back.

Mrs Bloxby came back with a tray with mugs of coffee.

'What's the gossip?' asked Agatha.

'Er . . . James was here when you were away.'

Agatha sat bolt upright. 'Where is he now?'

'I'm afraid I don't know. He only stayed for an afternoon. He said he was travelling abroad.'

'Rats!' said Agatha gloomily, all the old pain flooding back. 'Did you tell him where I was?'

'Yes, I did,' said the vicar's wife awkwardly. 'I told him where you were living in London and gave him your phone number.'

'He didn't call,' said Agatha miserably.

'He did seem in a bit of a rush. He sent his love.'

'That's a joke,' said Agatha bitterly.

'Now drink your coffee. I know it's early, but would you like something stronger?'

'I don't want to start down that road, especially for a creep like James,' said Agatha.

'Have you met your new neighbour?'

'No. I saw him when he moved in, I mean from a distance, but then I got the chance of this PR job and took off for London. What's he like?'

'Seems pleasant and clever.'

'What does he do?'

'He works in computers. Freelance. He's just finished a big contract. He says he's glad it's over. He was commuting to Milton Keynes and back every day.'

'That's a long haul. No murders?'

'No, Mrs Raisin. I should think you've had enough of those. There is a small mystery, however.'

'What's that?'

'Alf was recently asked to perform an exorcism, but he refused.' Alf was the vicar. 'Alf says he only believes in the divine spirit and no other kind.'

'Where's the ghost?'

'It's a haunted house in Hebberdon – you know, that tiny village the other side of Ancombe. It belongs to an old lady, a Mrs Witherspoon, a widow. She has heard strange voices and seen lights in the night. Alf has put it down to the village children playing tricks on the old lady and has suggested she call in the police. She did that, but they couldn't find anything. But Mrs Witherspoon sticks to her story that she is being haunted. So, do you want to investigate?'

Agatha sat for a moment and then said, 'No. I think Alf's probably right. You know, sitting here I've decided to stop rushing around, finding things to ward off boredom. Time I broke the pattern. I'm going to become domesticated.'

Mrs Bloxby looked at her uneasily.

'You? Do you think that's a good idea?'

'The garden's full of weeds and this rain can't go on forever. I'm going to potter about and do a bit of gardening.'

'You'll get fed up soon.'

'You don't know me,' said Agatha sharply.

'Possibly not. When did you make this decision?'

Agatha gave a reluctant grin. 'Five minutes ago.'

Her stubborn pride kept her from revealing that James's visit and the fact that he had not tried to contact her had hurt her deeply.

As the wet spring finally dried up, it did indeed look as if Agatha Raisin had settled into domesticity at last. Tired of lazy gardeners, she had decided to do the work herself and found it alleviated the pain she still felt over James. The ladies of the village of Carsely informed Agatha that her neighbour, Paul Chatterton, was a charming man but not at all sociable. For a moment, Agatha's competitive instincts were aroused, but then she thought dismally that men meant pain and complications. They were best left alone.

She was sprawled in a deck-chair in her garden one sunny day, covered in a careful application of sunblock and with her two cats, Hodge and Boswell, at her feet, when a tentative voice said, 'Hello.'

Agatha opened her eyes. Her neighbour was leaning over the garden fence. He had a thick shock of pure white hair and sparkling black eyes in a thin, clever face.

'Yes?' demanded Agatha rudely.

'I'm your new neighbour, Paul Chatterton.'

'So? What do you want?' asked Agatha, closing her eyes again.

'I wanted to say hello.'

'You've already said that.' Agatha opened her eyes and stared at him. 'What about trying goodbye?'

She closed her eyes again until she felt he would have fully appreciated the snub. She cautiously opened them again. He was still standing there, grinning at her.

'I must say you make a refreshing change,' he said. 'I've been besieged by village ladies since I arrived, and now I decide to be sociable, I happen to pick on the one person who doesn't want to know me.'

'Bother someone else,' said Agatha. 'Why me?'

'You're the nearest. Besides, I hear you're the village sleuth.'

'What's that got to do with it?'

'I read in the local papers that there's some old woman over at Hebberdon who is being frightened out of her wits by ghosts. I'm going over there to offer my services as a ghost buster.'

Agatha's recently dormant competitive instincts rose. She sat up. 'Come round the front and I'll let you in and we'll talk about it.'

'See you in a few minutes.' He waved and loped off.

Agatha tried to get to her feet, thinking that old-fashioned canvas deck-chairs like the ones in

13

Green Park in London had been expressly designed to make one feel old. She found she could not struggle out of it and had to tip it sideways and roll over on the grass to get to her feet. She gave it a furious kick. 'You're for the bonfire,' she said. 'I'll replace you with a sun-lounger tomorrow.'

She hurried into the house, stopping only in the kitchen for a moment to wipe the sunblock from her face.

Agatha hesitated before opening the door to him. She was wearing a faded house dress and loafers. Then she shrugged. Men! Who needed to bother about them?

She opened the door. 'Come in,' she said. 'We'll have coffee in the kitchen.'

'I'd rather have tea,' he said, trotting in after her.

'What kind?' asked Agatha. 'I've got Darjeeling, Assam, Earl Grey, and something called Afternoon Tea.'

'Darjeeling will do.'

Agatha put the kettle on. 'Aren't you working at the moment?'

'No, I'm between contracts. Going to take a brief holiday.'

Agatha leaned against the kitchen counter. Paul's intelligent black eyes surveyed her and Agatha suddenly wished she were wearing something more attractive, or, at least, had some make-up on. He was not strictly handsome, and yet there was something about that white hair

14

combined with black eyes in a white face and a long athletic figure which, she thought, would disturb quite a lot of women – except, of course, she reminded herself, Agatha Raisin.

'I believe my cottage once belonged to your ex-husband, James Lacey,' he said. The kettle began to boil. Agatha lifted down two mugs and put a tea-bag in one and a spoonful of instant coffee in the other.

'Yes,' she said. She stirred the tea-bag, lifted it out and put the mug down in front of him. 'There's sugar and milk in front of you.'

'Thanks. Why Raisin? Did you get married again?'

'No, that was my first husband's name. I kept on using it even when I was married to James. Are you married?'

There was a short silence while Paul carefully added milk and sugar. He stirred his tea. 'Yes, I am,' he said.

'And so where is Mrs Chatterton?'

Another silence. Then he said, 'Visiting relatives in Spain.'

'So she's Spanish?'

'Yes.'

'What's her name?'

'Um . . . Juanita.'

Agatha's bearlike eyes narrowed. 'You know what I think? I think you're not married at all. I think there isn't any Juanita. Look, I invited you in here, not to get into your trousers, but because I'm interested in this ghost thing.'

His black eyes sparkled with amusement. 'Are you usually this blunt?'

'When I'm being lied to, yes.'

'But there is a Juanita. She has long black hair –'

'And plays the castanets and has a rose between her teeth. Forget it,' snapped Agatha. 'So what do you plan to do about the haunting?'

'I thought I'd run over there and offer my services. Care to join me?'

'Don't see why not,' said Agatha. 'When shall we go?'

'What about now?'

'Okay. Finish your tea and I'll get changed.'

'No need for that. Your housewifely appearance might reassure Mrs Witherspoon.'

'Tcha!' said Agatha. She left the kitchen and ran upstairs. She put on a cool pink-and-white-striped shirtwaister dress and then carefully applied make-up. She longed to wear high heels, but the day was hot and swollen ankles would not look chic. She sighed and pushed her feet into a pair of low-heeled sandals.

She was half-way down the stairs when she realized she had forgotten to put on tights. A hot day minus tights would mean the straps on her sandals would scrape across her feet and the skin of her thighs under the short dress might stick to the car seat. She went back to her bedroom and struggled into a pair of tights labelled 'One Size Fits All', reflecting that whoever put that slogan on the packet had been thinking of a skinny fourteen-year-old. She looked in the mirror. The effort of putting on the tights in a hot bedroom had made her nose shine. She powdered it too vigorously and got a sneezing fit. By the time she had finished sneezing, her make-up was a wreck, so she had to redo it. Right! A last look in the full-length mirror. God! The buttons at the bosom of her shirtwaister were straining. She took it off and put on a white cotton blouse and a cotton skirt with an elasticated waist.

Fine. Ready to go. One more look in the mirror. Damn. She was wearing a black bra and it showed through the white cotton. Off with the blouse, on with a white bra, blouse back on again.

Resolutely not looking in the mirror this time, Agatha darted down the stairs.

'You shouldn't have gone to so much trouble,' said Paul.

'I haven't gone to any trouble,' growled Agatha.

'You were away ages and I thought . . . Never mind. Let's get going. You'd better take a pair of wellingtons.'

'Why?'

'Because there's still foot-and-mouth around and she may live near a farm and we might have to wade through disinfectant.'

'Right,' said Agatha. 'I've got a pair by the door. Whose car? Yours or mine?'

'I'll drive.'

His car was a vintage MG. Agatha groaned

inwardly as she lowered herself down into the low seat. She felt as if she were sitting on the road. He set off with a roar and Agatha's hair blew forward about her face.

'Why is it in films,' she said, 'that the heroine in an open car always has her hair streaming behind her?'

'Because she's filmed in a stationary car in a studio with a film of landscape rolling behind her and a studio fan directed on her hair. If it's bothering you, I can stop and put the top up.'

'No,' said Agatha sourly. 'The damage is done. Whereabouts in Hebberdon does this Mrs Witherspoon live?'

'Ivy Cottage, Bag End.'

Agatha fell silent as the countryside streamed past, the ruined countryside, the countryside destroyed by foot-and-mouth. If she had still been in London, she wouldn't have given a damn. But somehow she now felt she belonged in the countryside and what happened there affected her deeply.

Hebberdon was a tiny picturesque village nestling at the foot of a valley. There were no shops, one pub, and a huddle of cottages. Paul stopped the car and looked around. 'I'll knock at one of the doors and ask where Bag End is.'

Agatha fished out a cigarette and lit up. There was a hole where she guessed the ashtray used to be. Still, it was an open car. He could hardly object.

He came back. 'We can leave the car here. Bag End is just around the corner.'

Getting out of the car to Agatha was reminiscent of getting out of the deck-chair, but she managed it without having to roll out on the road.

They walked round into Bag End, a narrow lane with only one cottage at the end. Agatha took a final puff at her cigarette and tossed it at the side of the road. Paul retrieved it and stubbed it out. 'You'll set the countryside alight in this weather,' he complained.

'Sorry,' mumbled Agatha, reflecting that she was not really the countrywoman she had thought herself to be. 'How old is this Mrs Witherspoon?'

'Ninety-two, according to the newspapers.'

'She might be gaga.'

'Don't think so. Let's see anyway.'

Ivy Cottage was indeed covered in ivy which rippled in the summer breeze. The roof was thatched. Paul seized the brass knocker and gave it a good few bangs. After a few moments, the letter-box opened and a woman's voice shouted, 'Go away.'

'We're here to help you,' said Paul, crouched down by the letter-box. 'We'll lay the ghost for you.'

'I'm sick of cranks. Sod off!'

Paul grinned sideways at Agatha. 'Sounds like

a soul mate of yours.' He turned back to the letter-box.

'We're not cranks, Mrs Witherspoon. 'We really do want to help.'

'How can you do that?'

'I am Paul Chatterton with Agatha Raisin. We live in Carsely. We're going to spend a night in your house and catch your ghost.'

There was a long silence and then the rattle of bolts and chains. The door opened. Agatha found herself looking upwards. She had imagined that Mrs Witherspoon would turn out to be a small, frail, stooped old lady. But it was a giantess that faced her.

Mrs Witherspoon was a powerful woman, at least six feet tall, with dyed red hair and big strong hands.

She jerked her head by way of welcome and they followed her into a small dark parlour. The ivy clustered round the leaded windows cut out most of the light.

'So what makes you two think you can find who is haunting me?' she asked. Her head almost touched the beamed ceiling. Agatha, who had sat down, stood up again, not liking the feeling of being loomed over.

'It's worth a try,' said Paul easily. 'I mean, what have you got to lose?'

Mrs Witherspoon turned bright eyes on Agatha. 'You said your name was Raisin?'

'He did. And yes, it is.'

'Ah, you're the one from Carsely who fancies

herself to be a detective. Your husband ran off and left you. Hardly surprising.'

Agatha clenched her hands into fists. 'And what happened to yours?'

'He died twenty years ago.'

Agatha turned to Paul and began to say, 'Maybe this is a silly idea after all . . .' but he hissed, 'Let me handle it.'

He turned to Mrs Witherspoon. 'We would be no trouble,' he coaxed. 'We could sit down here during the night and wait.'

'Don't expect me to feed you,' she said.

'Wouldn't dream of it. We'll come about ten.'

'Oh, all right. I've lived in this cottage all my life and I am not going to be driven out of it.'

'What form do these hauntings take?'

'Whispers, footsteps, a sort of grey mist seeping under the bedroom door. The police have been over the place, but there's no sign of forced entry.'

'Have you any enemies?' asked Agatha.

'Not that I know of. I'm a friendly sort. Never anything about me to upset people.' She fastened her eyes on Agatha's face with a contemptuous look as if to imply that there was a lot about Agatha Raisin to get people's backs up.

Paul edged Agatha to the door, seeing she was about to burst out with something. 'We'll be back at ten,' he said.

'I don't think I want to help that old bitch,' she

21

railed, when they got into the car. 'Believe me, Count Dracula wouldn't even frighten that one.'

'But it is interesting,' protested Paul. 'As a child, didn't you want to spend the night in a haunted house?'

Agatha thought briefly of the Birmingham slum she had been brought up in. There had been so much earthly terror and violence that as a child she had little need to scare herself with things supernatural.

She sighed and capitulated. 'May as well give it a try.'

'I'll bring a late supper and a Scrabble board to pass the time.'

'A Ouija board might be better.'

'Haven't got one of those. What would you like to eat?'

'I'll eat before we go. Lots of black coffee would be a good idea. I'll bring a large Thermos.'

'Good, then. We're all set.'

They drove back into Carsely under the watchful eyes of various villagers.

'I saw Mrs Raisin out with that Paul Chatterton,' complained Miss Simms, secretary of the ladies' society, to Mrs Bloxby when she met her outside the village stores later that day. 'I don't know how she does it! Here's all of us women trying to get a look in and she snaps him up. I mean ter say, she's no spring chicken.'

'I believe men find Mrs Raisin sexy,' said the

vicar's wife and tripped off with her shopping basket over her arm, leaving Miss Simms staring after her.

'Would you believe it?' Miss Simms complained ten minutes later to Mrs Davenport, a recent incomer and now a regular member of the ladies' society. 'Mrs Bloxby, the wife of a vicar, mark you, says that Mrs Raisin is sexy.'

'And what prompted that?' demanded Mrs Davenport, looking every inch the British expatriate she had recently been – print dress, large Minnie Mouse white shoes, small white gloves and terrifying hat.

'Only that our Mrs Raisin has been driving around with Paul Chatterton and the pair of them looking like an item.' Under the shadow of the brim of her hat, Mrs Davenport's face tightened in disapproval. Had she not presented Mr Chatterton with one of her best chocolate cakes and followed it up with two jars of home-made jam? And hadn't he just politely accepted the gifts without even asking her in for a coffee?

Mrs Davenport continued on her way. The news rankled. In the manner of British expatriates who lived on a diet of rumours, she stopped various people, embellishing the news as she went. By evening, it was all round the village that Agatha was having an affair with Paul Chatterton.

At six o'clock that evening, Agatha's doorbell

rang. She hoped that perhaps it was Paul inviting her out for dinner. Detective Sergeant Bill Wong stood on the doorstep. Agatha felt immediately guilty. Bill had been her first friend when she had moved down to the country. She didn't want to tell him about the search for the ghost in case he would try to stop her.

'Come in,' she said. 'I haven't seen you for while. How are things going?'

'Apart from chasing and fining ramblers who will try to walk their dogs across farmland, nothing much. What have you been getting up to?'

They walked into the kitchen. 'I've just made some coffee. Like some?'

'Thanks. That's the biggest Thermos I've ever seen.'

'Just making some coffee for the ladies' society,' lied Agatha.

'I hear James was back in Carsely – briefly.'

'Yes,' said Agatha. 'I don't want to talk about it.'

'Still hurts?'

'I said, I don't want to talk about it.'

'Okay. How's the new neighbour?'

'Paul Chatterton? Seems pleasant enough.'

Bill's round face, a mixture of Asian and Western features, looked at her curiously. Agatha's face was slightly flushed.

'So you haven't been getting up to anything exciting?'

'Not me,' said Agatha. 'I did some PR work in London, but down here I've been concentrating on the garden. I made some scones. Would you like one with your coffee?'

Bill knew Agatha's baking was bad, to say the least. He looked doubtful. 'Go on,' urged Agatha. 'They're awfully good.'

'All right.'

Agatha put a scone on a plate and then put butter and jam in front of him.

Bill bit into it cautiously. It was delicious, as light as a feather. 'You've really excelled yourself, Agatha,' he said.

And Agatha, who had received the scones as a gift from Mrs Bloxby, smiled sweetly at him. 'You'll never believe how domesticated I've become. Oh, there's the doorbell.'

She hurried to open the door, hoping it would not be Paul Chatterton who might start talking about their planned vigil at the haunted house. But it was Mrs Bloxby.

'Come in,' said Agatha. 'Bill's here.' She hoped Bill had finished that scone.

But to her horror, as she entered the kitchen with Mrs Bloxby, Bill said, 'I wouldn't mind another of those scones, Agatha.'

'Oh, do you like them?' asked Mrs Bloxby. 'I gave Mrs Raisin some this morning because I'd made too many.'

'Coffee?' Agatha asked the vicar's wife.

'Not for me. The attendance at the ladies' society is not very good, so I called round to make sure you would be at it this evening.'

'I can't,' said Agatha, aware of Bill's amused eyes on her face.

'Why not?'

'I've got to see a man about some PR work.'

'Working again so soon? I thought you wanted a quiet summer.'

'Oh, well, it's just a little job.'

'What is it this time? Fashion?'

'It's a new anti-wrinkle face cream.'

'Really? Do you think those creams work?'

'I don't know,' said Agatha loudly. 'It's all too boring. Can we talk about something else?'

There was a silence. Agatha felt her face turning red.

'You're getting quite a name for yourself in the village,' teased Mrs Bloxby. 'It's all over the place that you and Paul Chatterton are an item.'

'Nonsense.'

'You were seen out in his car.'

'He was giving me a lift.'

'Oh, is your car off the road?'

'Look,' said Agatha, 'I was leaving to go to Moreton and he came out of his house at the same time and said he was going to Moreton as well and offered me a lift. That's all. Honestly, the way people in this village gossip.'

'Well,' said the vicar's wife, 'a lot of noses have been put out of joint by your apparent friendship with him. Why should you succeed when so many others have failed? I'd better go.'

Agatha saw her out and then returned reluctantly to the kitchen. 'You haven't let me have another of those scones yet,' said Bill.

'I must have made a mistake and given you one of Mrs Bloxby's scones instead of one of my own,' said Agatha, who, once she was in a hole, never knew when to stop digging.

'Then I'll have one of yours.'

Agatha went through the pantomime of opening an empty tin. 'Sorry,' she said. 'Mine are all finished. What a pity.'

She put another of Mrs Bloxby's scones in front of him.

'Have you heard of a Mrs Witherspoon who claims she is being haunted?' asked Bill.

'Yes, it was in the local papers.'

'And you didn't feel impelled to do anything about it?'

'No, I want a quiet life. She's probably gaga.'

'She's not. I went a couple of times to investigate. The police couldn't find anything. I've got this odd feeling you're hiding something from me, Agatha.'

'Don't be silly.'

'I mean, I ask you about this new neighbour of yours and you don't tell me he took you down to Moreton.'

'What is this?' demanded Agatha. 'The third degree?'

Bill laughed. 'I still think you're holding out on me. Well, I'm sure a bit of ghost-hunting won't hurt you.'

'I never said –'

'No, you didn't, did you? I would ask you about this face cream and where you are meeting this man, but I don't want to stretch your imagination any further.'

'Bill!'

He grinned. 'I'll see you around.'

Agatha sighed with relief when he had left and went upstairs to take a shower. She felt hot and clammy after all her lies.

Now what did one wear for ghost-hunting?

Chapter Two

By the time Agatha went downstairs that evening, she left the bedroom behind her in a mess. She had tried on just about everything in her wardrobe, veering from the chic to the shoddy, and had finally settled on wearing a pair of comfortable woollen trousers, a checked shirt and a cashmere sweater.

Don't get interested in men again, she told herself severely and looked so grim when she opened the door to Paul that he took a step back and asked her whether anything was the matter. 'No, nothing,' said Agatha. 'I'll get the coffee.'

'I forgot to tell you. Sometimes I prefer tea, and this is one of those sometimes.'

Agatha threw him a filthy look and went through to the kitchen and picked up the huge Thermos. At least all the coffee she had made should keep her awake.

'We'll take my car,' she said firmly. The evening was chilly and she did not relish the idea of bucketing through the lanes in Paul Chatterton's MG.

Outside, Paul loaded a picnic basket into Agatha's new Audi. 'You've brought a lot,' commented Agatha.

'I haven't eaten yet. Have you?'

'I had something,' lied Agatha. Somehow she felt guilty about having wasted so much time changing in and out of clothes and putting on full make-up with mascara and eye shadow and then wiping it off and replacing it with a lighter maquillage. Her stomach gave a rumble and she added quickly, 'But only a sandwich.'

'Just as well I've got enough for two,' he said.

Agatha drove off, wondering how many curtains in the village were twitching as they cruised past.

'Isn't this exciting?' said Paul.

'Yes,' said Agatha doubtfully. She didn't believe in ghosts. Old houses, such as her own and Mrs Witherspoon's, were full of creaks and noises. Ahead of her lay a sleepless night with a man she didn't really know.

They arrived at Ivy Cottage and unloaded the car. Mrs Witherspoon answered the door wearing a voluminous scarlet dressing-gown which clashed with her red hair.

'Oh, it's you,' she said ungraciously. 'Go into the living-room and settle yourselves. If you need the bathroom, it's the door off the landing. Otherwise, don't bother me, and don't wake me. I'm a light sleeper.'

'You'd think she didn't want us to find her

ghost,' grumbled Agatha after Mrs Witherspoon had retreated upstairs.

'Never mind. I'm going to eat.' Paul opened up the hamper, took out several plastic boxes, and plates and knives and forks. 'There's cold chicken, salad and French bread,' he said cheerfully. 'Help yourself, and then we'll have a game of Scrabble.'

Agatha ate gratefully and accompanied her plate of food with several cups of strong black coffee. Paul had brought a Thermos of tea.

'So what brought you to Carsely?' asked Agatha.

'A desire for somewhere pretty and quiet. I usually live in London but it's become so noisy and crowded and dirty. Besides, Carsely is only an hour and a half away, so it's not exactly isolated.'

'Have you always worked with computers?'

'Yes, I was lucky. I started right after university. I got in pretty much on the ground floor.'

'What exactly do you do?'

'I'm a programmer. What about you? Retired?'

'Mostly, although I still take the odd job. I had my own PR firm in London but I sold up and took *early* retirement,' said Agatha, stressing the word early.

'And how did you get into amateur detection?'

'By accident,' said Agatha. 'You know, things happen and I get curious.'

'How do you go about it?'

'Go around asking questions. The police don't

31

often have time to get to know people and people will talk more freely to a civilian than they will to the police.' Agatha had an impulse to brag, which she quickly suppressed. She had an uneasy feeling that Paul found her more amusing than attractive.

After they had finished, he neatly packed the plates away. So much for Juanita, thought Agatha. Bachelors are always neat and domesticated. She suddenly remembered James Lacey and felt a stab of pain. Her eyes filled with tears.

'What's the matter?' asked Paul.

'I bit my tongue by accident.'

'Nasty, that. Let's play Scrabble.'

He arranged the board and tiles on the table. He started. He put down 'xenon' on the board.

'That's not a word,' said Agatha crossly.

'It is, you know. It's a gas. Here!'

He took out a copy of the Oxford Dictionary and handed it to her. Agatha looked it up. 'Okay,' she said sulkily. The game progressed. Paul won easily. They started another. An old marble clock on the mantel ticked drearily and then its rusty chimes sounded midnight.

The time crawled by. Paul won two more games. 'I'm bored,' said Agatha.

'Why don't you have a sleep? I'll keep watch.'

'I'll stay awake a little longer. The house is very quiet. I wish we could do something amusing to pass the time.'

He smiled at her. 'Well, there is something we could do.'

Agatha felt a frisson of sexual tension. 'And what's that?' she asked.

'I've a pack of cards. We could play poker.'

'No, that's even more boring than Scrabble, and you only want to play to make me look as silly as you've made me look over the Scrabble board. Does Juanita really exist?'

'Of course she does.'

'So why isn't she with you?'

'I told you, she's visiting relatives in Spain.'

'So you did. It's getting cold in here. What's that?'

Cold white mist was beginning to seep under the living-room door. Agatha stared at it as it crept around their legs.

'Come on,' said Paul, getting to his feet. 'Someone's playing tricks. Nip upstairs and see if Mrs Witherspoon's all right and I'll search the downstairs.'

'Do I have to?'

'Go on.'

Paul opened the living-room door and crossed the small hall to the kitchen at the back. Agatha mounted the stairs, her feet feeling like lead. 'Mrs Witherspoon!' she called in a quavering voice and then louder, 'Mrs Witherspoon.'

A door at the top of the stairs opened and a terrible apparition stood there, tall and white, with a green face and staring red eyes. Agatha screamed. She tumbled down the stairs and yanked open the front door. She got into her car, fumbling for her keys. She was dimly aware of

Paul shouting something, but she'd had enough. She roared off and did not stop until she had reached her own cottage. She did not feel safe until she was in her own bed with the duvet pulled up over her ears. Despite her fear, she fell into a heavy sleep from which she was aroused two hours later by the phone ringing. Assuring herself that ghosts surely did not know how to use the telephone, she answered it.

Paul's voice sounded down the line. 'Could you come and pick me up? You left me stranded.'

'I saw an awful thing . . .' began Agatha.

'That awful thing was Mrs Witherspoon in a face pack. She's furious with you. You're not very courageous for a detective.'

'See you soon.' Agatha slammed down the phone. She dressed hurriedly and went out to set off again for Hebberdon, feeling like a fool. Paul was waiting for her on the doorstep.

'I'm sorry,' said Agatha as he packed the picnic basket in the car. 'But how was I to know it was her? And all that cold mist.'

'That, I am convinced, was nothing more than carbon dioxide gas. There's no sign of anyone having broken in and the windows were all closed and locked. She says no one else has a key, but they must have.' He got into the passenger seat. 'Anyway, you've blown it. She's so furious with you, she doesn't want to see us again.'

'I've said I'm sorry,' shouted Agatha, moving off. 'What else can I say?' He began to laugh. 'What's so funny?'

'You,' he spluttered. 'You should have seen your face.'

'Have you not considered,' said Agatha coldly, 'that if someone is ruthless enough to frighten that old woman to death, they might have wanted to put an end to us?'

'No, I don't think so. I wanted to find out if she had much money and who would inherit, but she told me to mind my own business. I think we should go over to Hebberdon later today and ask the locals about her.'

Agatha felt ashamed of herself, and that shame was making her cross and irritated. She did not like not being in control, but grudgingly admitted to herself that to refuse to go on investigating would be childish. 'All right,' she said ungraciously. 'What time?'

'Oh, we'll get some sleep first. Say, eleven in the morning?'

'Right.'

He began to laugh. 'You must admit, it was very funny. You ran off screaming like a banshee!'

'Drop it. I feel a fool.'

'Well,' he said, conciliating, 'who would expect old Mrs Witherspoon to go in for a face pack at her age?'

'That carbon dioxide gas. At least we know there's someone human behind it. It *was* carbon dioxide, wasn't it?' asked Agatha.

'It might be. But surely the police would have thought of that.'

'I don't know. This government has been closing down so many country police stations that the police that are left are overloaded with work. Anyway, tomorrow's another day.'

When they set out again the following morning, Agatha resolved that nothing about this 'ghost' would scare her again. But she felt rather shy of Paul. *He* did not seem to feel in the least awkward around *her*, but then why should he? Probably regarded her as some sort of middle-aged eccentric, all right for a bit of amusement, only good enough to play Dr Watson to his superior brain. Agatha mentally checked her appearance. She was wearing a scarlet cashmere sweater over a pair of jersey wool trousers and flat sandals. She edged the sweater down a bit over her stomach. Time for more exercise and diet. What a bore ageing was! Things drooped and sagged and bulged unless one worked ferociously on them. The flesh under her chin was really showing a slackness which alarmed her. She had slapped herself again under the chin sixty times that morning and had performed several grimacing exercises in order to try to tighten the flesh up, which had resulted in a red neck. She hoped the red had faded. And yet why should she mind what Paul thought of her appearance? Because he's a man, she thought dismally, and she was mentally tied to her generation who considered every man as a prospective lover.

'Here we are,' said Paul, cruising to a stop. 'What we want to suss out is whether Mrs Witherspoon is regarded as eccentric and also who would get the house if she died. I mean, someone must be trying to frighten her to death.'

'Then someone doesn't know her very well,' commented Agatha.

'She's got high blood pressure.'

'How do you know that?'

'I went to the loo and checked out her pills in the bathroom cabinet.'

'So where do we start?' asked Agatha, looking around.

'The pub, I suppose.'

They got out of the car. The pub, a small square Victorian building, was called The Railway Arms. 'Didn't know there was a station here,' said Agatha.

'There probably was in the days when trains stopped everywhere. The Hereford line is quite close.'

Agatha looked at her watch. 'It's early yet. Don't suppose it gets many people at any time.'

'It's a free house. Hasn't been bought up by a brewery yet. They probably get ramblers when there isn't a foot-and-mouth epidemic. Come on.'

'Aren't you going to lock your car?'

'No, it'll be all right.'

'I would if I were you,' said Agatha. 'I see you've got a CD radio fitted.'

'Oh, stop worrying and let's get started.'

They walked together into the pub. The walls, once white, were now yellow with nicotine. A few framed photographs of steam trains hung on them. There was a scarred wooden bar along one wall and a few wooden tables and upright chairs were dotted about. A man with a balding head and a large beer belly stood behind the bar.

'What'll you have?' asked Paul.

'Gin and tonic.'

'Right. I'll have a tomato juice. It's a bit early for me.'

'I haven't no ice,' said the barman.

'I would be amazed if you had,' said Agatha.

The barman put their drinks on the counter. 'Visiting?' he asked.

'We're both living over in Carsely,' said Paul. 'Funny, that business about Mrs Witherspoon. We read about it in the papers.'

'You don't want to pay no heed to that,' he said.

'Why?' asked Agatha.

'Because she's an old bitch what'd say anything,' remarked the barman.

'That's interesting,' said Agatha. 'But you strike me as a very intelligent man. Do you work here or are you the landlord?'

'I own this pub.' He stuck out a hand. 'Barry Briar's the name.'

Agatha took his hand. He held hers and leered at her.

'So, Mr Briar,' said Agatha, tugging at her

hand until he released it, 'do you mean Mrs Witherspoon made the whole thing up?'

'Course she did. She likes the attention, see? Afore this, her was always calling the police out for something or another.'

'Like reporting you for serving drinks after hours?' said Paul.

'There's that. But there's other things.'

'Like what?' asked Agatha. 'Here, let me buy you a drink?'

'Ta. I'll have a malt.' Briar helped himself to a double measure and Agatha reluctantly paid up. 'Like there's Greta Handy at Pear Cottage. Her got the satellite TV in and Mrs Witherspoon reported her to the council for defacing an old building and they made her take the satellite dish down. Then there's Percy Fleming, him at Dove Cottage. He's a writer. He had a shed put in his garden for a place to work. Said he could keep all his computer stuff and manuscripts, like, and use it for an office. Even had the phone put in. Tasty liddle place, it were. Mrs Witherspoon reports him to the council and says he hasn't asked for planning permission and it's got to go. He paid lawyers and got his way, but it cost him a mint.'

'Goodness!' said Agatha, looking suitably enthralled. 'Does she have any family?'

'She has a daughter, Carol, lives over Ancombe way. And a son. They never talk.'

'Why's that?'

'Well, Carol is in her late sixties and never

39

married. She says she never had a chance. Her mother scared them all off. When she got the courage to leave, it were too late, poor old cow.'

'So she made all this ghost business up?' asked Paul.

'Course she did. She likes the fuss. Police and newspapers running around.'

The phone rang in the back premises and Briar went to answer it. Agatha and Paul carried their drinks over to a table.

'So what do you think?' asked Paul.

'Seems like he's telling the truth,' said Agatha.

'What about that mist?'

'She probably faked that herself. Look, if she was really frightened, she would have been anxious for our help, but she was pretty reluctant.'

'Drink up and we'll try those two neighbours she riled up.'

Greta Handy was a small, round, muscular woman. Her thick grey hair was scraped up on top of her head and she was wearing a man's pullover with a pair of torn and faded jeans. When she heard the reason for their call, she invited them in. They stood helplessly in her low-beamed living-room, wondering where to sit. A large dog of mixed breed was stretched out on a sofa and somnolent cats occupied the two easy chairs. The stuffy air was redolent of cat and dog, and various bowls of half-eaten cat and dog food were spread about the floor on the hair-covered carpet. A large television set dominated the room. Agatha noticed a digital box on top of the video machine.

'So you got satellite after all?' she said.

'Yes, that silly old woman. What a fuss. The engineers just took the dish off the wall and put it on a stand in the shrubbery.'

'So what about this ghost business?' asked Paul.

'Load of rubbish, if you ask me. She's run out of people to make trouble for, so she made the whole thing up. I'm amazed the police ever listened to her. I went round there and told her, I said, "You ever interfere again and I'll stick the bread knife in you." So she calls the police. "Never said anything like that," I told them. I mean, you say things in the heat of the moment that you don't mean, but if I'd told them I'd actually threatened her, they might have arrested me. But she didn't bother me again.'

Outside, Agatha and Paul took grateful breaths of fresh air. 'May as well try the other one, the writer,' said Paul.

When they rang the bell at Dove Cottage, there was no reply. 'Perhaps we should go round the back,' suggested Agatha. 'He may be in his shed.'

They walked along a narrow path at the side of the low thatched cottage. The front garden had been a riot of flowers, but the back garden consisted only of a square of lawn and the shed. It was a square wooden structure with a double-glazed window. 'Sheds like these cost a lot,' said Agatha. 'I wonder what he writes.'

'Maybe he writes under another name, one we'd recognize.' Paul rapped on the door of the shed.

A tall, stooped man opened the door. He had thick silver hair worn long, a black velvet jacket open over a white shirt and silk cravat, and black velvet trousers. 'Go away,' he said in a reedy voice. 'I am not buying anything.'

'We're not selling anything,' said Paul. 'I am Paul Chatterton and this is Mrs Agatha Raisin. We spent last night in Mrs Witherspoon's house, trying to lay the ghost for her but without success. General opinion around here so far seems to be that she is making the whole thing up.'

'Come in,' said Percy. They walked up the shallow wooden steps and into an office-shed which looked a miracle of order. Neat files in different colours filled the shelves and a computer and printer stood on a metal desk. Percy sat beside the desk and waved Agatha and Paul into two hard chairs facing him. 'I am glad you have come to me,' he said, making a steeple of his fingers and looking wise – or trying to look wise, Agatha thought. 'I am a writer and I have a writer's eye for detail.'

Probably can't write very well and must have a private income, reflected Agatha. She knew from long experience that successful writers rarely glorified their trade.

'Do you write under your own name?' she asked.

'No,' he said proudly. 'I am Lancelot Grail.' He opened a drawer in his desk and took out a paperback which he handed to her. The cover showed a muscular man stripped to the waist, wielding an axe and being threatened by a dragon.

'Oh, now I know who you are,' lied Agatha, anxious to keep him helpful. 'So what can you tell us about Mrs Witherspoon?'

'To put it bluntly, she is a bitch from hell,' he said. 'Ah, I shock you by my plain speaking, Mrs Raisin, but that is what she is. She reported this shed to the planning officer and I had to employ a lawyer at Great Expense to clear things up. I told her to mind her own business in future and she told me to go and . . .' His face turned a delicate pink. 'Well, I will not sully your ears with such language. Of course she's making it all up. She's lonely and bored and her hobby is creating fuss and chaos.'

Agatha felt disappointed. Three people in this small village all said roughly the same thing. It looked as if there was no case and no case meant no more outings with Paul.

Paul got to his feet. 'Thank you for your time. So you really believe there's nothing in it? We

43

thought someone might be trying to frighten her to death.'

'Her! My dear fellow, all the dragons of Gorth could not frighten that old hag.'

'What's Gorth?' asked Agatha.

'It is a planet in my latest book. I would offer you a copy, but on the other hand, I feel people should buy my books and not expect free copies.'

'Wouldn't dream of it,' said Agatha in all sincerity.

As they approached his MG, Paul said ruefully, 'Nothing to investigate after all.'

Agatha looked at the parked car. 'I'm afraid there is.'

'What?'

She pointed to the soft top of the car, which Paul had left up. Someone had sliced through it with a sharp knife. Paul gave an exclamation and opened the car door. 'My CD player has gone.'

He looked wildly around. 'Who could have done this?'

Agatha took out her mobile phone. 'I'll call the police.'

Bill Wong made a detour into the ops room on his way out of police headquarters in Mircester. He rather fancied the new blonde recruit called Haley. She was just taking a call. He heard her say, 'Any units in the area of Hebberdon. Car-radio theft. Owner a Mr Paul Chatterton.'

Bill stood deep in thought while she gave further instructions. Not so long ago, a policeman from the nearest village would have been sent, but with the government closing so many rural stations, calls went out to patrol cars. Chatterton. Now that was Agatha's new neighbour and Hebberdon was that village where the old woman had been frightened by a ghost. So Agatha was investigating that business after all.

A patient policeman took down the details of the theft of Paul's radio-cum-CD player. 'We'll do our best, sir,' he said, finally closing his notebook. 'But in future, you should keep your car locked.'

'And what difference would that make?' demanded Paul angrily. 'They assumed it was locked anyway and just sliced through the roof. Someone must have seen something. It's such a small village.'

They turned and looked up the winding road and then down but nothing moved in the patchy sunlight. 'Let's try the pub,' suggested Agatha.

'Just leave the investigating to us,' said the policeman. 'I have your phone number, Mr Chatterton. We'll let you know if we find anything.'

He stood there until they drove off.

'I feel sick,' said Paul. 'I love this car.'

'Then you should take better care of it,' snapped Agatha.

'Are you always so insensitive and rude?'

They arrived back in Carsely in an angry silence. Before she got out of the car, Agatha tried to heal the breach. 'Look, Paul, I'm sorry I made that crack about you taking better care of your car.'

But he sat at the wheel, staring straight ahead.

Agatha climbed out and stomped off into her cottage. Rats, she thought. I've blown it. She walked through to the kitchen and opened the back door and let her cats out into the garden. She made herself a cup of coffee and followed them out and sank down into the deck-chair. Now what should she do? To tell the truth, she admitted to herself, she had rather enjoyed stealing a march on the other women of the village by cruising around with Paul Chatterton. She probably wouldn't have a chance to talk to him again. Now that there appeared to be no mystery to solve, he would probably take on another work contract.

The doorbell shrilled from the front of the house. She tried to struggle to her feet and ended up rolling the whole deck-chair to the side so that she fell out on to the grass. She hurried through the house. Please let it be Paul, please let it be Paul, went her mind. I'm sure it's Paul. She threw open the door.

Bill Wong stood on the step.

Agatha's face fell.

'Expecting someone else?' asked Bill.

'No, no. Come in. Another visit, and so soon! Come through to the garden. Coffee?'

'No, it's a flying visit.'

They walked into the garden. 'I'll bring out a chair,' said Agatha. 'Try the deck-chair,' she added, malicious in her disappointment. 'It's very comfortable.'

She carried out a hard kitchen chair. Bill settled himself in the deck-chair.

'I heard a report from Hebberdon that your neighbour's car was broken into.'

'And you came all the way here just for that!'

'I wondered what you two were up to. The only thing that would take you to Hebberdon, Agatha Raisin, is ghost-hunting.'

'Oh, well, you may as well hear it all. Okay, I'm sorry I didn't tell you, but I thought you wouldn't want me to interfere.'

'Quite right. Anyway, what did you find out?'

'Nothing much. I made a fool of myself.'

His brown eyes smiled up at her from the depths of the deck-chair. 'You? Never! What happened?'

'Paul persuaded Mrs Witherspoon to let us spend the night. At first it was all very quiet and boring. Then this cold mist began to creep into the room. I ran upstairs to see if Mrs Witherspoon was all right. There was this horrible sight with a green face and a long white gown. I ran

47

screaming out of the house. Paul phoned me to say that the apparition had been Mrs Witherspoon in her nightie with a face pack on. No wonder she looks so sour. You're not supposed to sleep with a face pack on.'

Bill chortled with laughter and stroked Boswell, who had jumped on to his lap.

'Anyway,' Agatha went on, 'we went there today to ask around. Mrs Witherspoon doesn't want to have anything to do with us. We were told by three of the neighbours that she was only doing it to get attention.'

'And you believe that?'

'I think that old ratbag would do anything to upset people.'

'Maybe. The police sat it out in that cottage a couple of nights but nothing happened. This cold mist . . .?'

'Probably carbon dioxide, dry ice; they use it on stage sometimes.'

'Well, that's something. Didn't you find that odd?'

'After what the neighbours say, I suppose she was playing tricks on us. The stuff's pretty easy to get, presumably.'

The doorbell rang. 'Excuse me,' said Agatha. This time, she did not expect it to be Paul, but it was the man himself who stood there.

'Oh, Paul,' said Agatha faintly. 'I did say I was sorry.'

'It's all right,' he said, his black eyes gleaming

with excitement. 'I've just had a call from the police. They've found my radio.'

'Come in. I've got a detective friend here.' She led the way through to the garden. 'Bill, this is Paul Chatterton. Paul, Detective Sergeant Bill Wong.'

Paul sank down on to the grass beside Bill. 'Yes, the police have just phoned. They found my car radio and CD player in a dry ditch beside where my car was parked.'

'That's odd,' said Bill. 'Maybe someone came along and whoever stole it just dropped it.'

'Or Mrs Witherspoon, anxious for more attention, did it herself,' said Agatha.

'Come on, Agatha,' protested Bill. 'She's an old lady!'

'A very fit old lady and very strong,' said Agatha.

'Anyway,' said Paul, 'I'm going over to Mircester to identify it and pick it up. Feel like coming?'

Bill noticed the way Agatha's face lit up, and his heart sank. Paul was a very attractive man. Bill didn't want to see Agatha getting hurt again.

'Wait a minute,' he said. 'Let's finish talking about this haunted-house business.' Bill's almond-shaped eyes gleamed. 'Was there any more mist?'

'No, none at all.'

'Did you search around? Any canisters?'

'Nothing.'

'Any wet patches on the floor outside the room where you were sitting?'

'I didn't look. Why?'

'Dry ice does not really need to be wet with water to give off a visible vapour; it will freeze water vapour in the air near it, producing visible vapour all by itself. However, if you add water, it works at an accelerated rate and you'll get a lot more mist.'

'So you think there might be something in this?' asked Paul.

'Probably not. Funnily enough, the police on both occasions came to the conclusion that she wanted attention. I've got to go.' To Agatha's irritation, he rose out of the deck-chair in one fluid movement. Bill was young, in his late twenties. Oh, God, her inability to get out of that hell-chair must be the first creaking signs of age.

Agatha walked him to the door. 'Be careful,' whispered Bill.

'Of what? Ghosts?'

'Of falling in love again.'

'I won't. He says he's married.'

'Let's hope that damps your ardour.'

Agatha retreated into the house. 'Going to the loo,' she shouted. She nipped quickly up the stairs and put on fresh make-up.

'We'll take my car,' she said to Paul when she made her appearance in the garden again.

'Fine.' He rose to his feet. 'I think I'll buy myself an old banger for driving around. I'd better take care of my MG in future.'

Honestly, thought Agatha, I bet he's even got a name for the damn thing.

Chapter Three

'I would have thought they'd want to keep your CD player for forensics,' said Agatha as she drove competently along the Fosseway to Mircester.

'It's a minor crime,' said Paul. 'They won't bother. I wonder if Mrs Witherspoon is schizophrenic.'

'What makes you say that?'

'In some of the initial newspaper reports it referred to crashes and bumps and things falling down. Poltergeists are people with the knack of telekinesis. They can move objects with their minds. Usually it's a three-year-old or someone in their forties, don't ask me why. It's something to do with the pineal gland. But schizophrenics also can manage it.'

'See any pills in her bathroom cabinet to do with that?'

'Nothing but diuretics, pain-killers and high blood pressure pills.'

'Oh, well,' said Agatha, 'case closed. It

seems as if she only wanted to draw attention to herself.'

'I don't know about that,' he said slowly. 'She's a crusty old lady but I wouldn't have thought she would have needed the attention. She struck me as being pretty self-contained.'

They both fell silent. Agatha thought, should I ask him out for dinner? A nice candle-lit dinner? Eyes meeting across the table. 'Agatha, I would like us to be more than friends. Dear Agatha . . .'

'Are you listening to me?' Paul's voice suddenly cut through her dreams.

'No, I wasn't. What did you say?'

'About this evening . . .'

Ah, two minds with but one single thought.

'What about this evening?' asked Agatha in a husky voice.

'If you're up to it . . . Oh, I don't know . . .'

'I'm up to anything,' said Agatha, her hands suddenly clammy on the wheel. When did she last shave her legs? Did her toenails need cutting?

'I thought it might be an idea to sit outside the cottage tonight and watch it. I mean, if someone else other than Mrs Witherspoon is behind these hauntings, we might see someone hanging about the house. In fact, it might be exciting. Be a good chap and say yes.'

'I am not a chap,' said Agatha, irritable in her disappointment. Why did fellows never speak the script one had written for them?

But going on with the investigation meant going on in his company. 'All right,' she said.

'Grand. We'll pick up the machine and then get a bite to eat. My treat.'

Agatha's spirits, which had plummeted, soared up again.

While Paul was led off to identify his CD player and sign the relevant papers, Agatha asked the sergeant at the desk whether she could use the loo. Once inside a white-tiled institution-alized toilet smelling strongly of disinfectant, she opened her capacious handbag and got to work, cleaning off the make-up she had so recently applied and adding a new coat of foundation, powder, blusher and eye shadow. Then she sprayed herself liberally with Ysatis and returned to the reception area. Where would he take her for dinner? Surely somewhere nice.

Paul finally reappeared, accompanied by Bill Wong and a small blonde policewoman whom Bill introduced as Haley. 'I've asked them to join us,' said Paul cheerfully. 'Bill says the Dog and Duck does a good meal.'

Agatha stifled a sigh. Bill's taste in food was appalling.

The Dog and Duck was one of those pubs that the modern taste for smart bistro-style hostelries had passed by. A snooker table dominated one end of the room. Fruit machines flashed and blinked in the dim smoky light. The bar was crowded with plain-clothed and uniformed police and CID. A menu was chalked up on a board. Agatha gloomily read it. Lasagne and chips, curry and chips, egg, sausage and chips, hamburger and chips, fish and chips, and quiche and chips. So much for her idea of a romantic evening.

Bill started to ask Agatha how various people in Carsely were getting on and when she had finished replying, she noticed, with extreme irritation, that Paul appeared to be flirting with Haley, who was giggling appreciatively.

Haley had a round face and narrow blue eyes. Her hair was what Agatha privately described as 'cheap blonde' – but what man had ever been put off by that?

'Paul's ever so clever,' said Haley. 'He's promised to come round to my place one day and help me with my computer.'

'Oh,' said Agatha sharply. 'I thought all you police were computer-literate these days.'

'I only know the basics,' said Haley. She pulled out a notebook. 'Here! Let me write down my address and phone number for you.'

Agatha and Bill watched her gloomily as she wrote down her details and handed them to Paul.

'How old are you?' asked Agatha abruptly.

'Twenty-seven,' said Haley. She giggled again. 'Ever so old.'

'You've a long way to go before you are as old as either me or Paul,' said Agatha sweetly.

'Terrible for a woman to be old,' said Haley.

'I mean, doesn't matter so much for men. I fancy older men. Here's our food.'

The food was as awful as Agatha had thought it would be. She had ordered fish and chips, thinking that even this pub could not muck up such a simple dish, but the fish was thin and dry and the chips of the frozen variety.

She watched with horrified fascination as Haley dredged her lasagne in ketchup and began eating with every sign of relish.

Bill and Paul had both ordered sausage, egg and chips.

Haley ate steadily and then leaned back with a sigh of satisfaction. 'That was good.'

She surveyed Agatha. 'I hear you're a bit of a Miss Marple.'

A vision of Miss Marple as played on television rose before Agatha's eyes and she began to feel ancient.

'I have done some detective work, yes,' she said.

'Anything at the moment?'

'Came to nothing,' said Agatha, pushing her plate away. 'We were supposed to be investigating a haunted house.'

Haley clutched Paul's arm and let out a shriek. 'I'm ever so afraid of ghosts.'

'Have you seen one?' asked Paul, smiling down at her.

'No, but my gran has. She was up in this old hotel in the Highlands of Scotland once and she woke up during the night and saw a man standing at the foot of her bed.'

'Was he wearing a kilt?' asked Agatha cynically.

'Yes, he was. And he looked ever so fierce. My gran, she got the Gideon Bible out of the drawer beside the bed and held it up and he disappeared.'

'Gosh!' said Paul. 'How scary. I remember hearing a story about . . .'

He proceeded to relate several ghost stories while Haley alternately giggled and shrieked and clutched his arm more tightly.

Agatha was relieved when Bill finally looked at his watch and said, 'I have to go.'

'I don't,' said Haley, and Agatha's heart sank.

'But we do,' said Paul firmly. 'It's been a delight to meet you, Haley.'

'You will let me know when you're coming round?'

'Absolutely.'

'What a disgusting meal,' said Agatha as they drove off.

'Yes, wasn't it? Anyway, we'd better get back and prepare for our night watch.'

'What time do you want to set out?'

'About midnight.'

'Do you really think we should?'

'Why not? Let's have a go anyway. Is Haley Bill's girlfriend?' asked Paul.

'Not yet, and possibly not ever after the way you went on tonight.'

'Oho! Jealous, Agatha?'

'Don't flatter yourself, Humbert Humbert. You didn't give Bill a chance.'

'*She* didn't give Bill a chance. Don't let's quarrel. I think we should park outside the village and wear dark clothes.'

Agatha looked at her watch as they neared Carsely. Eleven o'clock. Just time to get something to eat to make up for having barely touched the fish and chips, and then get changed.

She resolved not to torture herself any more by trying on outfit after outfit. It was time to grow up and move on. Dressing for men meant never feeling secure, never feeling comfortable.

She had eaten a microwaved curry, without ever reflecting on the irony of a woman such as herself who could sneer at pub food and yet hardly ever prepared a decent meal. She put on a pair of black trousers, a black sweater, flat shoes and the minimum of make-up and was ready when Paul rang her doorbell.

Paul thought briefly that there was something rather sexy about grumpy Agatha. Her skin was good and her mouth generous, her bust and hips very beddable, but then he concentrated on the night ahead.

Fortunately it was quite warm and the sky above was clear.

Like Agatha, he was dressed in black trousers and a black sweater. 'I hope you've got something for your head,' she said. 'That white hair of yours shines out like a beacon.'

'I've got something. We'll need to use your car again. I'm taking mine to the garage tomorrow. I've ordered another top for it, but I'll also buy something to run around in, the type of old banger I won't care about too much if it gets vandalized.'

'You should get a security alarm put in that old MG of yours,' said Agatha.

'I probably will.' He put a heavy bag in the back seat of Agatha's car and then got into the passenger seat at the front.

'What's in the bag?' asked Agatha.

'Some refreshments and a pair of binoculars. It's going to be a long night.'

As they approached Hebberdon, Paul said, 'Slow down. There's a good place. That farm entrance under the trees. Reverse into it.'

Agatha went in, nose-first. 'Don't you know women drive forwards, not backwards?'

They got out of the car. 'We have to walk through the village to get to her place,' said Paul. 'But I don't think anyone will be awake.'

That did seem to be the case as they walked past silent dark cottages. Even the pub showed no signs of life. 'There's a field opposite with a pretty high hedge,' said Paul. 'We'll settle down there and watch.'

They squeezed through a gap in the hedge. 'Ground should be dry,' said Paul. 'Look, if we settle down here, there's a big hole in the branches right opposite. We'll get a good view.'

Mrs Witherspoon's cottage was all dark. Somewhere an owl hooted. Paul opened up his bag and took out a bottle of malt whisky and two glasses. 'Drink?'

'Maybe I shouldn't,' said Agatha. 'I'm driving.'

'The effects will have worn off before morning. Go on.'

'All right, just a small one. Have you ever noticed,' said Agatha, 'how many people urge one to drink? I mean, it's always drink. Say you don't like fish. No one says, "Oh, go on, have one. Why not half a fish? Go on, why not a fish finger?" No, it's always drink, like drug pushers.'

'You only had to say no,' said Paul mildly. 'Cigarette?' He pulled out a packet.

'You smoke!' exclaimed Agatha with all the delight of one member of an endangered species meeting another.

'From time to time.'

They sipped their whisky and smoked and stared across at the cottage. Nothing moved, nothing happened.

'What happened to your marriage?' asked Paul, filling up her glass again.

'It just fell apart. James was a genuine copper-bottomed bachelor. We didn't get on. What about your marriage to the supposed Juanita?'

'Well, she's in Spain a lot and I'm here, but we get on pretty well when we meet up.'

'Children?'

'No. You?'

'No, none.'

'So what brought you to the Cotswolds?'

'It's pretty,' said Agatha. 'It's pretty everywhere you look. London's not the same. It's getting violent and dirty. Of course, I notice all the faults when I go up on business but maybe if I still lived there, I wouldn't pay all that much attention to what's wrong. Sometimes Carsely seems a bit boring and I get restless, but something always happens. There's murder and mayhem here, just like in the cities.'

'And what about men?'

'What about them?'

'I mean, do you have a lover?'

'No,' said Agatha curtly.

'And yet your reputation in the village seems to be that of a sort of Cotswolds femme fatale.'

'There are women in Carsely who've got nothing else to do but invent stories about me. I'm just a stuffy middle-aged woman.'

He filled her glass again. Agatha felt dimly that she ought to protest but the whisky was soothing and warming and she had always maintained she had a strong head for drink.

'I wouldn't call you stuffy.' He had put on a black woollen cap to eclipse his white hair. His black eyes glinted in the darkness. He leaned forward and surprised her by planting a warm kiss on her lips. Agatha gazed up at him, mesmerized. He bent his head towards her again. A twig snapped.

He straightened up and whispered, 'That came from across the road.'

Agatha tried to get up and stumbled and fell. Her head swam. 'Shhh!' He deftly put bottle, glasses and binoculars back in his bag. He pulled her to her feet. 'Let's get over there.'

He nimbly eased through the gap in the hedge. Agatha weaved after him. There was a metal dustbin outside the cottage gate, ready for collection. Agatha stumbled into it and the whole thing rolled over with a crash.

'Now that's torn it.' Paul seized hold of her as a light went on in an upstairs window. 'Run!'

With his arm around her waist, supporting her, he hustled her through the village and out to where her car was parked. He took the keys from her and unlocked the doors. Despite her drunkenness, Agatha noticed he had had the forethought to bring his bag along with him. 'I'll drive,' he said.

He drove off, not accelerating until he was well away from the village. 'I shouldn't have drunk so much,' mourned Agatha.

'My fault,' he said. 'I'm sure there was someone there.'

'Could have been a fox or a sheep.'

'Maybe. Get some sleep and we'll try again another time.'

'So you think he's lying about being married?'

asked Mrs Bloxby the next day. 'Why should you think that?'

Agatha shuffled her feet like a schoolgirl. 'Well, he kissed me.'

'Oh, *Mrs Raisin*. Really. You said you had both been drinking. The fact that he is married does not necessarily stop him from making a pass at you. Haven't married men ever made a pass at you before? You must have attended a lot of boozy functions during your PR work.'

'But that was London and this is a village!'

'And when did village life ever bestow sainthood on a married man? Wishful thinking can be very dangerous. I mean, before you left him, did he kiss you again or say any endearments?'

'No-o. But we'd both had a fright, what with me knocking the dustbin over. Anyway, where is this mysterious wife?'

'Probably in Spain, just like he said.'

'You do spoil things,' remarked Agatha crossly.

'I care for you. I don't want to see you getting hurt.'

Agatha sighed. 'You can't fall in love without getting hurt.'

'Now, listen to me, falling in love is an addiction for you. Your trouble is you do not really like yourself half enough. So the minute you find your brain empty of some obsession or other, you race around trying to fill the gap.'

'Thank you for sharing that with me, Oprah Winfrey.'

'I mean it. Oh, never mind. I didn't mean to upset you. I'll say a prayer for you.'

Agatha shifted awkwardly in her chair, suddenly embarrassed. Mrs Blockley hardly ever pulled what Agatha privately thought of as 'the God bit' on her.

I mean, saying that she was trying to fall in love. Ridiculous!

But when Agatha left the vicar's wife, she could feel the first chill wind of reality creeping into her brain. Better to forget about that kiss.

As the day dragged on, she began to wonder about his marriage. She hadn't been inside his cottage. Maybe he had photographs of the two of them. Maybe there were some Spanish things lying around. She could call on him. Why not? He had said they would try again another time.

She fed her cats and made herself a couple of sandwiches for lunch and then headed for the cottage next door.

Paul looked surprised to see her, but said, 'Come in. Have you any more news?'

'Nothing. I wondered when you wanted to try again.'

'I don't know,' he said uneasily. 'Want a coffee?'

'Please.'

He went through to the kitchen. Agatha's eyes roamed around the room. No photographs. Crowded bookshelves, nice leather winged armchair, chintzy sofa and easy chair, a computer desk with computer and printer, a pleasant oil painting depicting a rural scene over the fire-place and a faint smell of tobacco smoke. James would have hated that, thought Agatha. He never liked her smoking in the house. Agatha felt herself relax. It was a bachelor's house, of that she was sure.

Paul came back with a tray with mugs of coffee. 'I know you like yours black,' he said. 'I can't talk very long. I'm waiting for a phone call.'

'About work?'

Hesitation. Then he said, 'Yes, something like that.'

Uneasy silence while Agatha sipped her coffee and tried to think of something to say.

The phone rang. 'Do you mind . . .?' said Paul.

Agatha stood up. 'See you soon,' she said.

She left, feeling empty. Mrs Bloxby was right. That kiss had meant nothing. Still, there was nothing in that cottage living-room to show he was married.

For the next two days, Agatha mooched around, feeling time lie heavy on her hands. She had seen nothing of Paul. She had tried to phone him, but there had been no reply. On Saturday evening she set out for the vicarage to attend a meeting of the ladies' society, glad of something to do.

Mrs Bloxby opened the proceedings, Miss Simms read the minutes, and Agatha went off into a dream where Paul Chatterton was telling her he loved her and only jerked out of it when she realized she was being addressed. 'The catering?' Mrs Bloxby was saying, looking directly at her. 'Fund-raising for Alzheimer's Society?'

'What?' asked Agatha.

'You should be interested,' sniggered Mrs Davenport, implying that Agatha showed signs of having the disease.

'I'm sorry,' said Agatha. 'My thoughts were elsewhere.'

'We're joining forces with the Ancombe Ladies' Society on June tenth to raise money. It's to be a sale of work. We need someone to do the catering.'

'Okay, I'll do it,' said Agatha, thanking her stars that she had enough money to hire a good catering firm.

'Excellent!' The meeting moved on and Agatha relapsed back into her dreams.

During the tea and cakes afterwards, Agatha found herself accosted by Mrs Davenport. 'A word of warning,' she said. 'About Mr Chatterton. He is married, you know.'

'That's what he says. But it's only to keep the old frumps of the village from bothering him,' said Agatha.

'Like you?' said Mrs Davenport sweetly and moved away.

Agatha eyed her narrowly. Mrs Davenport had gone back to wolfing the delicate little ham sandwiches supplied by Mrs Bloxby. Agatha slid off into the kitchen, where more sandwiches and cakes were laid out on the kitchen table, ready to be brought into the drawing-room. Agatha opened the fridge and searched around until she found a bunch of hot chilli peppers. She quickly sliced them up and put them on as many of the little sandwiches as she could and then picked up the plate and carried it back into the drawing-room.

'You shouldn't have bothered,' said Mrs Bloxby. 'I made too many. They've all started on the cakes.'

'A pity to waste such good food,' said Mrs Davenport, sailing up, her massive bust making her look like the figurehead on a ship. 'I'll take a few.' She took about six on to her plate.

Agatha slid to the back of the crowd. There were two remaining chilli pepper sandwiches. She popped them in her handbag.

Mrs Bloxby swung round in alarm as Mrs Davenport, red in the face, gasping and spluttering, staggered about the room. The plate with most of the sandwiches still uneaten had fallen to the floor. One of them had broken open, revealing the chilli peppers. While the other women rushed to get Mrs Davenport a glass of water, Mrs Bloxby looked around the room for Agatha Raisin.

But there was no sign of her.

Agatha decided on Sunday that it was time she

67

attended church again. The fact that Paul might be there, she told herself, was nothing to do with it. She owed it to Mrs Bloxby to put in the occasional appearance.

The day was cloudy and overcast, threatening rain. She put on a soft wool suit and her Burberry over it, collected her umbrella and made her way to the church where the bells were pealing out under the lowering sky.

The church was full. Although the government kept saying the foot-and-mouth plague was under control, pyres of dead animals still smoked and smouldered across Britain, and, as usual in times of adversity, people went to church.

Agatha managed to squeeze into a pew near the front and then regretted it. If she had sat at the back of the church, she would have been able to see if Paul was at the service.

She kept twisting her head around until she had to give up because Mrs Davenport was in the pew directly behind her and looking daggers.

So while most of the congregation sang the hymns, said the prayers and listened to the sermon, Agatha Raisin wrapped herself in a dream of announcing her engagement to Paul Chatterton in *The Times*, where with luck James Lacey would read it.

Finally it was over. Agatha got to her feet. 'I want a word with you,' boomed Mrs Davenport.

'Not now,' hissed Agatha, pushing her way down the aisle. She could see Paul's white head of hair ahead of her.

Outside the church, she stood suddenly stock-still. For Paul was standing talking to the vicar, his arm around the waist of a small pretty woman with long dark hair.

Realizing that people were pushing to get past her, Agatha moved reluctantly forwards. It couldn't be. Could it?

She suddenly didn't want to know. A crowd had gathered around Paul and the woman with him. Agatha tried to edge past but Paul, taller than the people surrounding him, saw her and shouted, 'Agatha!'

The crowd parted. Agatha walked slowly forward. 'Agatha, my wife, Juanita. Darling, this is my neighbour, Agatha Raisin.'

'How nice to meet you,' said Agatha with a crocodile smile. Juanita was young, possibly in her early thirties, and that *was* young to the likes of Agatha Raisin. Her golden skin glowed with health and her wide brown eyes were fringed with thick lashes. The only consolation – and it wasn't much – that Agatha could notice was that her long black hair was thick and coarse. She was wearing a neat little black suit which emphasized her generous bust and her trim waist.

'Are you staying long?' asked Agatha.

Juanita laughed and said with a pretty accent,

'I think it is time I spent as long as possible with my husband.'

'I'm just next door,' Agatha forced herself to say. 'Call on me if I can be of any help in any way.'

Juanita thanked her and Agatha made her way home, legs as heavy as lead, mind snapping, 'You old fool.'

She was blindly fumbling in her handbag for her house keys when a voice behind her said, 'You look awful. Been to a funeral?'

Agatha swung round. Roy Silver, Agatha's ex-employee who now worked for a big public relations firm in the City, stood there.

'Roy!' exclaimed Agatha, more delighted to see him than she had ever been before. 'Come on a visit?'

'Just for the day.' He gave her a peck on the cheek.

'Well, come in and make yourself at home.'

Roy followed her into the kitchen. 'I should use the living-room more often,' said Agatha. 'I'll just feed the cats and we'll go through and have a drink. You're looking well.'

Roy did indeed look marginally better than his usual weedy self. He was wearing a sweater, checked shirt and jeans and his limp hair had recently had a conventional cut. 'In fact,' said Agatha, bending down and filling two feed bowls, 'you look quite respectable. No studs, no earrings. Is this the new image?'

'I'm handling a baby food account and they're very square.'

'And no raincoat. Did you drive down?'

'Yes, the roads aren't too bad on Sundays. How's foot-and-mouth?'

'Hanging on.' Agatha straightened up. 'Come through. What'll you have?'

'A G and T, thanks. Small, I'm driving.'

'Okay, sit down and I'll get some ice.'

'So,' said Agatha after she had fixed their drinks, 'What brings you?'

'I'll be honest with you,' said Roy.

'Makes a change.'

'Still taking on freelance work?'

'From time to time. What have you got?'

'You know Dunster and Braggs?'

'The chain store, yes. Everyone knows them.'

'They're launching a new line, Youth Fashion. Boss wants your ideas.'

'I know what Youth Fashion means,' said Agatha gloomily. 'Same as Mr Harry clothes. Cheap clothes made out of T-shirt material and all of it made in the sweat-shops of Taiwan.'

'We'd pay well. He wants you to start as soon as you can.'

'If you wait until I pack a suitcase, you can drive me up to London.'

Roy looked at her in surprise. 'I never thought it would be this easy. What gives?'

'Just bored, that's all.'

'No murders?'

'Not one. Oh, there was this house that was

71

supposed to be haunted, but it turned out to be just some old lady trying to get attention. I'll go and pack.'

Agatha was gone for a month, taking her cats with her this time. Paul Chatterton landed a short contract with a firm in Milton Keynes, which meant he had to leave early in the morning and did not return until late in the evening. Mrs Bloxby called on Juanita as part of her parish duties and found the lady highly discontented.

'It's so boring here,' was Juanita's complaint. 'I want to go back to Madrid. Paul could get work there. I should have married someone nearer my own age and a Spaniard. That's what my mother said. If only I'd listened to her.'

'Mr Chatterton will soon have finished his contract,' said Mrs Bloxby, 'and then he'll be able to take you about. Maybe you could go to London for a visit.'

'I don't want to go to London,' said Juanita. 'I want to go to Madrid.'

Outside, the rain was drumming down, making puddles in the grass. 'It's sunny in Madrid.'

In vain did Mrs Bloxby try to rope her in to take over the catering duties that Agatha Raisin had so cavalierly forgotten about. All Juanita would say was that it was boring.

After three weeks, she arrived at the vicarage

carrying her suitcase and asked for a lift to the station. Mrs Bloxby pleaded with her to at least stay until Paul came home that evening. Juanita said stubbornly that she had made up her mind. If Paul wanted her, he knew where to find her.

So Mrs Bloxby drove her to the station and waved goodbye to her as she boarded the London train.

Now Mrs Raisin's dreams will start up again, thought Mrs Bloxby crossly. I only hope Mr Chatterton decides to follow his wife.

But when she spoke to Paul that evening, he heard her in silence, looking angry and resigned.

'Why don't you go after her?' suggested Mrs Bloxby.

'My wife insists on living with her mother and three brothers. We had a flat of our own in Madrid for four weeks after we were married and then we moved to London. She would not settle and kept making excuses to go home. At first I kept going over there, but I could not get her to move out of the family home again. She's thirty-two and yet they all treat her like a child and so that's the way she behaves. The last time she said she had heard the English countryside was pretty and why didn't we live there? So I bought this cottage, but this is the result. Damn women. Where's Agatha, by the way?'

'Working in London.'

'I might be going up there for a day. Know where's she's staying?'

'No,' lied the vicar's wife and silently asked God to forgive her. Agatha had phoned her with the address of the service flat she would be staying in.

Agatha was happy to be back. Her conscience, never usually very active, had nonetheless continued to jab her over promoting clothes which were shoddy and badly designed. Summer had arrived at last and the taxi bearing her home from Moreton-in-Marsh station cruised down under the arches of green trees which leaned over the Carsely road.

After she had released the cats from their travelling boxes into the sunshine of the garden, she took a deep breath of sweet air and then went indoors to unpack.

At least the time in London had got Paul Chatterton firmly out of her head. Juanita might be fun to know, a change anyway from nasty trouts like Mrs Davenport.

The expensive block of service flats she had been staying in – expensive mainly because they allowed pets – had boasted a gym and Agatha had made good use of it. Her waist was trim and her stomach flat – well, nearly. She changed into a pair of sky-blue shorts and a blue-and-white gingham blouse and walked along to the post office-cum-general stores to buy groceries.

She was paying for the groceries when she noticed a bundle of local papers on the counter.

The headline on the top one said: OWNER OF HAUNTED HOUSE FOUND DEAD. Agatha bought a copy and hurried home with it. She stacked away her purchases and settled down at the kitchen table to read the story.

Mrs Witherspoon had been found by her daughter lying at the bottom of the stairs with her neck broken. Daughter Carol Witherspoon, aged sixty-seven, of Holm Cottage, Ancombe, said that she had not heard from her mother and became worried because her mother usually phoned her every Friday. She had let herself into her mother's house with her key and had found her dead. Mrs Witherspoon had reported to the police on several occasions that her home was haunted. Agatha pushed the paper away and sat deep in thought. The staircase, she remembered, had been carpeted, and the stairs themselves, shallow.

Of course something or someone might have frightened Mrs Witherspoon so much that she had lost her footing. Even so, how did she manage to break her neck? She had shown no signs of suffering from brittle-bone disease. Her back had been ramrod-straight.

The doorbell rang. Agatha went and opened the door and looked up into Paul Chatterton's black eyes. 'Oh, it's you,' she said weakly. 'Come in.' She peered round him. 'Where's your wife?'

'Gone back to Spain.'

'Oh.' Agatha walked ahead of him into the

kitchen. He noticed idly that she had long smooth legs, not a varicose vein in sight.

'You've lost weight,' he said.

'There was a gym at the flats I was staying at. I used it as much as possible. Coffee?'

'You've forgotten. Tea, please.'

Agatha plugged in the kettle. 'Would you do me a favour, Paul? Just before I left I bought four decent garden chairs. They're stacked in the shed at the bottom of the garden. Here's the key. Could you bring out two of them?'

'Sure.' He took the key and headed off out into the garden to a rapturous welcome from the cats.

Agatha made tea for him and coffee for herself and carried both into the garden to where Paul had set up two garden chairs with comfortable cushioned seats and backs.

'Did you have time to read about Mrs Witherspoon?' he asked. 'I find it all very odd.'

'So do I,' said Agatha, suddenly happy. 'What are we going to do about it?'

Chapter Four

Agatha Raisin listened to her conscience, which was currently telling her not to have anything further to do with Paul. The rest of her mind was just glad to see him. Not for a moment would she admit to herself that she dreaded loneliness. She prided herself on being a self-sufficient woman. She only knew that she was glad that he was back, glad his wife was in Spain, and glad that the investigation had started up again.

'The problem,' said Paul, 'is where to begin.'

'There's the daughter,' said Agatha. 'She lives over at Ancombe. But it's too soon after her mother's death to go calling.'

'I wonder when the funeral is,' said Paul. 'I'd like to see who turns up for it. Now the daughter didn't like her mother, so a call from us wouldn't shock her or upset her. We can just say we're friends of her mother and that we would like to pay our respects at the funeral.'

'We could do that. I'll get the phone book.'

'Better if we call in person.'

'I know, but I'll get the phone book and find out her address.'

Agatha came back after a few minutes. 'I've written it down. She lives at Four Henry Street. I know Henry Street. It's in a council estate at the far end of the village.'

'No time like the present. Let's go.'

'I'd better change.'

'Pity,' he murmured, eyeing her legs.

'Are you a flirt, Paul?'

'Just an appreciative comment.'

Agatha went upstairs and changed into a long summer skirt, remembered him looking at her legs and changed into a short one, thought that might look as if she was giving him a come-on, and changed back into the long skirt, worried that it looked frumpy, and put on a blue linen dress with a medium-length skirt, redid her make-up and finally went downstairs.

'You were ages,' complained Paul. 'I nearly went up to look for you.'

'I'm here now,' saw Agatha, reddening slightly under his gaze.

'So let's go.'

Most of the council houses on the estate had been bought by the residents from the government, and to advertise their new home-owning status, some had added 'picture' windows and fake Georgian porticoes. Number Four, unlike its neighbours, had a neglected air. The garden was weedy and the front door and window frames were badly in need of fresh paint.

Paul pressed the bell and then knocked on the door. 'I don't think the bell works,' he said.

The door was opened by a large, bony woman with grey hair. A strong smell of whisky emanated from her and her faded blue eyes were red-rimmed and watery.

'What?' she demanded.

'We were friends of your late mother,' said Paul. 'We wondered whether you could tell us the time of the funeral so we could pay our last respects.'

'I don't know. Ask Harry. He's in charge of arrangements.'

'Who's Harry?'

'My brother.'

'Where can we find him?' asked Agatha.

'Oh, come in. I'll write the address for you. He's over in Mircester. I haven't seen him in years.'

They followed her into a dingy living-room. Agatha's sharp eyes noticed a half-empty whisky bottle and glass behind a chair. Carol went over to a table by the window and began to search among a pile of papers until she found a notebook. 'Here it is,' she said, opening it. 'Number Eight-four Paxton Lane.' She scribbled the address on a piece of paper and handed it to Paul.

'When did you last see your mother?' asked Agatha.

79

'You mean before I found her dead?'

'Yes.'

'The Saturday before that. I always went over on Saturdays, God knows why. All I ever got was a mouthful of abuse. Did Harry go near her? You bet your life he didn't. Didn't give a monkey's for her and yet she leaves it all to him.'

Carol began to cry, tears rolling down her face and cutting channels in the thick make-up she was wearing. They waited in awkward silence until she finally blew her nose and wiped her eyes. 'Mother never forgave me for leaving,' she said. 'Wanted me to stay there like a slave. Well, I showed her!'

'Were you ever bothered by the hauntings your mother was complaining about?' asked Agatha.

'No. I think she dreamed all that up to try to get me to go back and live there. I feel sick about the whole thing. I've got to go to the inquest.'

'When's that?' asked Paul.

'Mircester Coroner's Court tomorrow at ten in the morning. How come you're friends of hers? She didn't have any friends.'

'We called on her to help lay her ghosts,' said Paul.

'Then you're fools. There weren't any ghosts. She was my mother, God rest her soul, but she was a nasty old bitch.'

'So that's where we'll go tomorrow,' said Paul.

'It'll be interesting to see who turns up at the coroner's court.'

'Aren't we going to see this Harry?'

'He'll be there tomorrow.'

'But we might not get a chance to speak to him,' said Agatha.

'Maybe he'll be at work.'

'With his mother so recently dead? Oh, if you've got better things to do . . .'

'Don't sulk. Let's go.'

'He's a lot better off than his sister to live here,' commented Paul when Agatha parked in Paxton Lane. 'These little gems of houses are all seventeenth-century.'

'I wish we'd asked her what he worked at, just in case he isn't at home,' said Agatha.

'Too late now. Come on.'

There were no gardens in front of the houses, only small paved areas, but all were decorated with bright tubs of flowers.

Paul rang the bell. A curtain twitched at the side of the door and then after a few moments, it was opened.

'Mr Harry Witherspoon?' asked Paul.

'Yes, who are you?'

'We are friends of your mother's. We would like to pay our respects at the funeral.'

He was surprisingly short in stature, compared to his tall mother and sister. He had thick grey hair and a round face criss-crossed with red veins. A small toothbrush moustache decorated his upper lip. His grey eyes were wary.

'The funeral's on Friday,' he said. 'Saint Edmund's in Towdey. At eleven o'clock. No flowers.'

Agatha remembered that Towdey was a village near Hebberdon. The door began to close.

'Might we have a word with you?' asked Paul.

The door reluctantly opened. 'Come in, but just for a minute. Have to get round to the shop.'

'And what shop's that?' asked Agatha as they followed him in.

'Mircester Antiques in the Abbey Square.'

The parlour into which he led them was furnished with various pieces of antique furniture. Paul recognized a pretty George III table and a Sheraton cabinet.

Harry did not ask them to sit down. He took a position in front of the marble mantelpiece. 'Who exactly are you?'

'I am Paul Chatterton,' said Paul, 'and this is Agatha Raisin. We visited your mother to see if we could catch the ghost for her.'

'Oh, that nonsense. She was old, you know, and I think her mind was going. Her death was a mercy in a way.'

'When did you last see her?'

'I dunno. Might have been Christmas.'

'That long,' exclaimed Agatha.

His eyes narrowed.

'I don't see what I do or when I last saw my

mother is any business of yours. Now, if you don't mind . . .'

'Not much there,' remarked Paul as they got into the car.

'You know, we're both assuming it was murder,' said Agatha. 'Maybe it was just an accident after all. Let's go round to police headquarters and see if Bill is in.'

At police headquarters, they were put into an interview room and told to wait. To their surprise, after a long wait two detectives entered, neither of whom was Bill.

'Isn't Bill here?' asked Agatha.

'This is our investigation,' said one. 'I am Detective Inspector Runcorn and this is Detective Sergeant Evans. We gather from DS Wong that the pair of you spent a night at Mrs Witherspoon's house at Hebberdon to see if you could lay the ghost for her. Is that true?'

'Yes,' said Paul.

Runcorn consulted notes in front of him. 'You are Paul Chatterton and you are Mrs Agatha Raisin?'

They both nodded.

'Okay,' said Runcorn. 'I gather you didn't find any ghosts.'

'That's right,' said Agatha. 'But there was this weird white mist, you know, like dry ice.'

'We'll start with Mr Chatterton,' said Runcorn. 'Did you think the old woman was gaga?'

'On the contrary,' said Paul. 'I thought she was very clear-minded and remarkably fit for her age.'

'Not infirm or tottering in any way?'

Agatha butted in. 'Those stairs she's supposed to have fallen down,' she said eagerly, 'they were shallow and well-carpeted.'

'In a minute, Mrs Raisin. Now, Mr Chatterton. Were you both there all night?'

Agatha relapsed into a sulky silence.

'I was there longer than Mrs Raisin,' said Paul.

'Why was that?'

Paul grinned. 'Mrs Raisin had a fright and ran away.'

'What frightened her?'

'I . . .' began Agatha.

Runcorn held up his hand. 'Mr Chatterton?'

'When the mist began to seep in from under the door, I told Mrs Raisin to run up the stairs to see if Mrs Witherspoon was all right. Mrs Witherspoon appeared in a long night-gown and green face pack. Mrs Raisin screamed, ran out of the house and into her car and drove home. I had to phone her later and ask her to come back and pick me up.'

The three men laughed heartily, bonding together in that moment in their shared amusement at the idiocy of women.

'And after Mrs Raisin had left, did anything else happen?'

'No, Mrs Witherspoon told me to let myself out, that she never wanted to see either of us again. I waited for a bit and then, as I said, I phoned Mrs Raisin.'

'Interesting, that.'

'What I think . . .' began Agatha desperately.

Both detectives rose. 'Thank you for your time, Mr Chatterton. We'll be in touch if we can think of anything else to ask you.'

'Just wait one sodding minute!' howled Agatha Raisin. 'I am not the invisible woman. I have solved cases for you before. This is the twenty-first century. How *dare* you all go on as if I don't exist and have nothing to contribute? Where is Bill Wong?'

'Lunch break,' said Runcorn. He held the door open for them and as Paul passed him, gave him a sympathetic pat on the shoulder.

'You weren't much help,' raged Agatha outside.

'Calm down. You couldn't really have added anything, could you?'

'I could have asked a lot of useful questions.'

'Such as?'

'Such as, who apart from daughter Carol had a key? Is there any other way into the house? It's very old. There could be a secret passage.'

'You're romancing, Agatha.'

'No, I am not!' she howled, causing several passers-by to turn and stare.

'Remember the Roundheads and Cavaliers?' asked Agatha, lowering her voice. 'All around us are old places with secret rooms and passages. I remember hearing there was one old place over

85

near Stratford and they discovered when they were lining the chimney that there was a secret room half-way up the inside of the chimney. Also, how much is the house worth? It's a thatched two-storeyed cottage, and very roomy inside. It's got beams and an ingle-nook fireplace in the living-room, all those little features that so delight estate agents.'

'I went through to the kitchen when you went upstairs,' said Paul. 'There's a very large extension been built on to the back of the house.'

'Furthermore,' pursued Agatha, 'it really gets my back up when I am ignored because I am a woman.'

'Never mind. Let's try that awful pub. Bill might be there and you can fire all your questions at him.'

Bill was there, tucking into a plate of greasy egg and chips. Agatha sat down while Paul went to the bar to get them drinks and launched into a bitter tirade about her treatment.

Bill heard her out and then said mildly, 'There's nothing I can do about it, Agatha. It isn't my case.'

'But you know something about it?'

'Maybe.'

'Who has keys to the house?'

'The daughter. No one else.'

'What about son Harry, who gets everything?'

'He says he doesn't have a key. When the hauntings started, Mrs Witherspoon got all the locks changed. She gave a key to Carol, not to Harry.'

'Why?'

'I gather Harry only called round infrequently and phoned before he did so.'

'What's his financial situation like?'

'They're looking into that.'

'Oh, are they?' Agatha's bearlike eyes gleamed. 'So they're not sure about it being an accident?'

'I think they're just checking out all the possibilities. It's a quiet time at the moment, otherwise they might not have become so curious.'

'The stairs were shallow and carpeted.'

'I heard that. There's something else.'

Agatha looked over at the bar. Paul was still busy trying to get the barman's attention. She suddenly wanted to know a few facts he didn't.

'What else?'

'She was evidently offered quite a large sum of money for the place, from Arkbuck Hotels.'

'Go on. For a cottage?'

'It's not only quite a large cottage but there are several acres of ground at the back belonging to Mrs Witherspoon. I gathered they planned a sort of expensive country retreat with a genuine Tudor cottage front and a new building, faked-up Tudor, at the back. But she turned down their offer.'

'Did she leave a lot of money?'

'She left close to a million pounds, plus stocks and shares.'

'The old bitch!' exclaimed Agatha. 'Her poor daughter lives in a run-down council house.'

'Agatha, Agatha. I suppose it's useless of me to tell you to stop poking your nose into police cases.'

Paul returned with the drinks in time to hear the last remark. 'No use at all,' he said cheerfully. 'Here's your drink, Agatha. Bill tell you anything?'

'Not much we didn't know,' said Agatha.

'I've got to get back,' said Bill. 'See you.'

'So what *did* he say?' asked Paul.

Agatha fought a silent war with herself. Why shouldn't she keep the information to herself and investigate herself, as she had done in previous cases? But he was wearing a sky-blue linen shirt open at the neck, and his silver hair and black eyes were such an alluring combination.

She caved in. 'Buy me lunch and I'll tell you.'

He looked up at the menu on the blackboard.

'No, you don't,' said Agatha. 'Not here!'

He grinned. 'All right. There's a French bistro on the other side of the square that's supposed to be pretty good. Come on.'

Agatha was hungry but found to her disappointment that the bistro still favoured nouvelle cuisine, tiny amounts of food exquisitely arranged on beds of that vegetable that Agatha so loathed – rocket.

'Stop grumbling,' said Paul, 'and tell me what you've got.'

Agatha relayed what Bill had told her. 'Great!'

exclaimed Paul when she had finished. 'When we get home we'll look up the headquarters of this hotel chain and go and see them.'

'Won't take us long to finish,' said Agatha gloomily. 'It's about a mouthful per course.'

When the bill arrived, Paul blinked a little at the cost of the meal, only glad that they had not had any wine. 'You and I are in the wrong jobs, Agatha,' he said as they left the restaurant. 'We should open a restaurant and starve the customers at great expense.'

'Bloody French,' muttered Agatha, still hungry.

'You're a racist, Agatha.'

'Not I. Anyway, the French are about the last race on earth you can insult because they don't give a damn what anyone says about them.'

Back in her cottage in Carsely, Agatha went through the London business directories without finding the headquarters of Arkbuck Hotels. 'Try the Internet,' said Paul.

Agatha switched on her computer. After a few moments, she said, 'I've got them. They're in Bath.'

'Well, that's not too far from here. Let's go.'

When they reached Bath, the terraces of Georgian houses were gleaming white under a darkening sky. The head offices of Arkbuck Hotels were situated in an elegant house in the Royal Crescent.

'Posh,' murmured Paul. 'I expected something a bit seedy.'

They walked into the reception area where an efficient grey-haired lady sat behind a Georgian desk, the sort of woman who, before the advent of computers, Agatha thought, could type eighty words a minute on an old Remington.

Paul introduced them and said they were interested in finding out about the bid for Mrs Witherspoon's cottage in Hebberdon.

Agatha expected to be told that everyone was busy, but to her surprise the receptionist said, 'I think Mr Perry is free.'

'Who is Mr Perry?' asked Agatha.

'Our managing director. Wait here.'

She walked up an elegant staircase. Paul studied photographs of the firm's hotels on the walls of the reception area. 'Doesn't look as if there's anything sinister about this lot,' he said. 'Converted manor houses, that sort of thing.'

The receptionist came down the staircase again, followed by a leggy secretary, who said, 'Come with me. Mr Perry will see you now.'

The secretary was wearing a very short skirt. Agatha noticed Paul eyeing the long legs walking up the staircase in front of them and felt a stab of jealousy. It just wasn't fair on middle-aged women. If she eyed up a young man she would be considered a harpy. But a man of the same age, provided he had kept his figure, would never be regarded with the same contempt.

The secretary led them through her office on the first landing and opened a door, ushered them in, and closed it behind them.

Mr Perry was a man in his fifties with a smooth, glazed face, small grey eyes, and large bushy eyebrows. He was impeccably tailored and he rested his manicured hands on the desk as he rose to meet them. 'What can I do to help you?' he asked in an Old Etonian accent, and Agatha's inferiority complex gave a lurch somewhere in the region of her stomach. She sometimes wondered if it was the inferiority complexes of people like herself that kept the British class system alive and well, rather than any behaviour of the upper classes. I mean, why *should* she feel inferior?

She realized with a start that Paul had said something and both men were now looking curiously at her. She shut her mouth, which had a distressing tendency to droop open when she was worried about something.

'Agatha?' prompted Paul.

'What?'

'I was just explaining to Mr Perry the reason for our interest in Mrs Witherspoon's cottage. And why don't you sit down?'

Agatha sat down in a chair facing Mr Perry.

'What you are really saying,' said Mr Perry, 'is that you believe there's something fishy about the old woman's death. You learned we had been trying to buy the house from her and thought, aha, sinister hotel chain will go to any lengths.'

91

'Something like that,' said Agatha, too taken aback to be anything other than honest. 'But that was before we came here. It all seems very respectable.'

He looked amused. 'The reason we wanted the place was because of the acreage at the back, and that, combined with the age of the house, made it seem ideal for our purposes.'

'But how did you even know about the place?' asked Agatha. 'I mean, you wouldn't know about that land at the back unless someone had told you.'

'Exactly.'

'So who told you?'

'I don't remember all the details. I did not approach Mrs Witherspoon myself. But we'll have the file somewhere.' He pressed a button on the intercom. 'Susie, get me the file on . . .' He looked at Paul. 'Name?'

'Ivy Cottage, Bag End, Hebberdon.'

'That's Ivy Cottage, Bag End, Hebberdon,' said Mr Perry into the intercom.

Agatha eyed a large glass ashtray on Mr Perry's desk. 'Mind if I smoke?'

'Not in the slightest. Would you like coffee?'

'Please.'

He pressed the intercom again. 'After you've found the file, Susie, bring us some coffee.'

'Does she mind that?' asked Agatha curiously.

'Mind what?'

'Being asked to make coffee?'

'Oh, no, we're a very old-fashioned firm.'

Susie came in and handed her boss a file.

Mr Perry opened it. 'Now, let me see. Ah, yes, we have a letter here. From the son, Harry Witherspoon.'

'Indeed!' exclaimed Agatha, her eyes gleaming with excitement.

'We were misled. We were under the impression that it was his to sell. He sent us photographs of the house and grounds.'

'It's his to sell now,' said Paul.

'I don't think we would want it. Ah, Susie. Coffee. Excellent. Just put the tray on the table.'

Agatha looked curiously at Mr Perry's face. Had he had plastic surgery? He looked up and caught her staring. 'I was in a car crash,' he said. 'They did quite a good job on my face, but not quite natural, don't you think?'

Agatha turned red with embarrassment. 'Looks fine to me,' she said gruffly. 'Why wouldn't you want the cottage?'

'It would take a great deal of restoration, and a cottage like that is a listed building. I could not see us getting planning permission. It has quite a history. Our man found out about it when he was doing his research. During the Civil War, that is Roundheads and Cavaliers, a certain Cavalier, Sir Geoffrey Lamont, fled the Battle of Worcester and took refuge there. It was rumoured he was carrying a fortune in jewels and gold with him. He did not know that his host, Simon Lovesey, had become a Cromwell sympathizer, and Lovesey betrayed him. Sir Geoffrey was hanged on Tower Hill.'

'And what happened to his fortune?' asked Agatha.

'Nobody seems to know. Shortly after betraying him, Lovesey died of consumption, which was what they called tuberculosis in those days.'

They helped themselves to coffee and talked about the price of houses until Mr Perry said he had an appointment in a few minutes and so they took their leave.

'Do you think there is buried treasure?' asked Agatha excitedly as they drove back.

'Not for a moment.'

'Oh, you! No romance in your soul. I'd like to search.'

'Well, you can't. I am not breaking into Ivy Cottage.'

'We might not need to break in. Look, when we go to the funeral, Harry's bound to have laid on some sort of reception at the house.'

'So?'

'So we join the other mourners and I get the key out of the front door and take it to a locksmiths, nip back and replace the original.'

'I think there's an easier way,' said Paul. 'I'm sure Harry will put the house up for sale as soon as the funeral is over. All we need to do is to wait a few days, find out which estate agent, and say we want to look the house over. In the meantime, it might be an idea to find out more about the history of the house. But don't go dreaming of buried treasure. If there had been anything, it would have been found ages ago. There might be a secret way into the house.'

'Let's go and see Mrs Bloxby and find out if there's a historical society which might have details about Ivy Cottage,' said Agatha.

'There's a historical society in Towdey,' said Mrs Bloxby. 'Do you know Towdey?'

'I know it's quite near Hebberdon,' said Agatha, 'but I've never actually been there.'

'It's quite big, a bit like Blockley. Used to be a mill town in the eighteenth century. I don't know who runs the society, but you could drive over there and ask.'

'We'll do that,' said Agatha. 'I suppose we'd best go to the inquest tomorrow. Bound to be a verdict of accidental death.'

But Agatha and Paul were in for a surprise.

The following morning found them both sitting at the back of the coroner's court in Mircester.

'There's a jury,' exclaimed Paul.

'Don't they always have one?' asked Agatha.

'Not always. The coroner summoned a jury, and the very inquest means the police aren't satisfied about the cause of death.'

'But I thought they always had an inquest when there's a sudden death and the deceased hadn't visited their doctor recently.'

'Shhh! Here's the coroner.'

Agatha stifled a giggle. The coroner looked as if *he* were dead. He was a tall thin man with a cadaverous face and stooped shoulders. His skin was yellowish and he gave a brief smile to the jury that looked more like a rictus.

The first witness was the policeman who had arrived on the scene at the same time as the ambulance. He said he found the deceased lying at the bottom of the staircase with her head at an awkward angle. She was in her night-clothes. The ambulance arrived at the same time. The body was examined for signs of life. None were found. Mrs Witherspoon's daughter had found her mother lying at the foot of the stairs and had summoned the emergency services.

Had the policeman suspected foul play? No, he said. The daughter, Miss Witherspoon, had said her mother suffered from high blood pressure and had probably had a seizure. Mrs Witherspoon's doctor, Dr Firb, had been summoned, but had refused to sign the death certificate.

The next on the witness stand was Dr Firb. He said that he had refused to sign a death certificate, preferring to wait for the police pathologist's report. 'Did you think the death suspicious?' asked the coroner.

'Not really,' said Dr Firb. 'But the circumstances seemed odd. She was admittedly an elderly lady suffering from high blood pressure, but she was very good about monitoring her blood pressure and taking her pills, and remarkably fit. I could see no signs of a stroke. Her neck appeared to have been broken. I assumed that was because of the fall but I wanted to be sure.'

There were various other questions regarding the late Mrs Witherspoon's mental and physical health which the doctor answered at great length while Agatha stifled a yawn. The coroner's court was hot and dusty. The long Palladian windows looked as if they had not been washed since the eighteenth century and only weak shafts of sunlight penetrated the grime.

Agatha's eyes began to droop. Soon she was asleep and only woke when Paul nudged her in the ribs an hour later and muttered, 'You're snoring.'

'Eh, what?' said Agatha loudly.

All eyes turned on her and she blushed. Carol Witherspoon was weeping on the stand.

'I do not want to prolong your ordeal,' said the coroner gently. 'I understand you went over to see your mother as usual?'

Carol scrubbed her eyes fiercely with a damp handkerchief.

'Yes, I did,' she said loudly. She glared around the courtroom until her red-rimmed eyes focused on her brother, Harry. 'And it's more than he ever did!'

'To whom are you referring?'

'My brother. Harry. Never bothered about her, hardly ever went to see her and she leaves

97

the lot to him! Well, I tell you this. He probably killed her!'

'I understand you are overwrought, Miss Witherspoon, but I would advise you to be careful with what you say.'

A lone reporter from a local paper, who had been yawning on the press bench, straightened up eagerly and began to scribble furiously.

'I'm saying it all looks odd to me,' howled Carol, now beside herself with rage. 'His business is on the rocks. Have you found out about that?'

'Remove the witness,' said the coroner.

A policewoman led the enraged Carol away from the witness stand.

'You've missed the best bits,' hissed Paul.

The coroner addressed the jury. 'You will disregard the accusations of the last witness. You have heard the various reports. It appears that Mrs Witherspoon, despite her age, was fit and well up until the time of her death. Before that, she had felt herself threatened by mysterious hauntings. The pathologist has stated that the deceased died of a broken neck. It might appear that Mrs Witherspoon died of a fatal fall down the stairs of her home, Ivy Cottage, in Hebberdon. Nonetheless, there was a black bruise on the front of her neck, commensurate with a sharp blow to that region of the body. The forensic report states that there were no fingerprints on the banister. The steps were thickly carpeted. Had Mrs Witherspoon fallen, she would surely have clutched at the banisters at some point to try to break her fall. Neither could the forensic team find any marks anywhere on the staircase which might match the fatal wound on her neck. You may retire to consider your verdict.'

The jury took only fifteen minutes to come to their decision. 'Murder by person or persons unknown.'

Agatha looked around the court for Harry Witherspoon, but he had disappeared.

'He can't sell the house now,' whispered Paul. 'Not until they find out who did it.'

Back in Carsely, Agatha said, 'It's all so obvious.'

'What is?' asked Paul. 'It's begun to rain and your cats are out in the garden. Will I let them in?'

'Open the door and they'll come in if they want. They're odd cats. They like rain. Obvious? I mean, it's obviously Harry who did it. He must have known he was due to inherit everything. His business is in trouble, Mother is old but looks likely to go on for a good few years.'

'Don't let it stop us from looking for other suspects.'

'Like who?'

'Percy Fleming.'

'What! The fantasy writer? Why him?'

'Just a thought. Maybe he got carried away with dislike of her and thought he was one of the characters in his books, Thor the Avenger, or something.'

'Wait a bit,' said Agatha. 'We're forgetting the hauntings. I can't see Harry messing about with dry ice and bumps in the night. Why would he want to drive her out of a valuable property he knew he stood to inherit?'

'Could be he wanted to frighten her to death,' said Paul.

'He knew her. She was his mother. He must have known it wouldn't be easy to frighten her. I feel restless,' said Agatha. 'Let's have something to eat and drive over to Towdey.' She opened the lid of a large freezer chest and pulled out several frosted packets and tried to scrape the ice off them to see what they were.

'Never mind,' said Paul quickly. He was sure the stuff Agatha was looking at had been in that freezer chest for years. 'We'll go now. There's bound to be somewhere in Towdey we can get a meal. I've got a car.'

'I know. The MG.'

'No, I got one for running around.'

The cats came in and wound their wet bodies around Agatha's legs. 'Shut the door before they get out again,' said Agatha. She picked up her handbag. 'Let's go.'

The village of Towdey was buried down in a fold of the Cotswold hills. The sun had come out again and mellow terraces of Georgian houses gleamed in the watery yellow light. Paul's car, an old Ford Escort, crunched over a mat of straw at the entrance to the village, left there from the days when it had been soaked in disinfectant at the height of the foot-and-mouth epidemic.

Paul followed the sign directing them to the centre of the village. 'Oh, look,' he said. 'There's a pub and it's got a menu on a blackboard outside.'

He parked in front of the pub and they both got out and studied the menu. 'Whatever happened to cheap village meals?' moaned Agatha. 'It's got things like sea bass and fillet steak at awful prices. I don't feel like eating a grand meal.'

'Let's try it anyway,' said Paul. 'Maybe they've got a bar menu inside with simpler things.'

The pub was Tudor, older than the surrounding eighteenth-century buildings. It was low-beamed and dark inside. A barman with an accent like Inspector Clouseau asked them what they wanted. Paul explained that they wanted a light snack and they were told to go through to the public bar, all with that hard-eyed look and slightly curled lip that the French do so well.

The public bar was across a stone-flagged passage from the lounge bar where the 'posh' meals were served.

The lounge bar had been empty but there were a good few people in the public bar. It was a long low room with a bare wooden floor and several tables and chairs. There was no one behind the bar but there was a bell on it with a little sign saying RING FOR SERVICE. Paul rang. Inspector Clouseau appeared.

'Ye-e-es?' he drawled.

'The cheap menu, please,' said Paul, becoming irritated.

A plastic laminated card was handed to him. Paul read out the brief menu: 'Cod and chips, lasagne and chips, egg and chips or chicken curry.'

'Prices?' asked Agatha.

'Extraordinary.'

'High?'

'Very high for the junk listed here.'

Paul handed the menu back. 'Forget it,' he said.

Clouseau flounced off.

'We'll go somewhere else later,' said Paul.

'How on earth can they survive?' demanded Agatha angrily as they walked outside. 'I mean, the pub isn't even on the tourist route.' She half turned back. 'Maybe it's a front for something.'

'One case at a time,' said Paul, drawing her away. 'Let's walk along a bit. There might be a shop and we can ask about the historical society.'

They walked along past rows of cottages. There were no gardens at the front but there were climbing roses hanging in front of the doors of some, growing out of tubs.

'There's a shop,' said Paul. 'Towdey Grocery and Post Office.'

But the shop was closed. 'Must be half-day.'

Paul peered in the window. 'Aren't some British shopkeepers amazing. They seem to have learned nothing from the Asians.'

'Look!' Agatha pointed to one of the cards in the window.

Among cards offering gardening services, baby-sitting, second-hand lawn-mowers, washing machines and bicycles was a neat card headed TOWDEY HISTORICAL SOCIETY. Underneath was typed: 'Roundheads and Cavaliers. Historical discussion on the royalist connections of Towdey in the Seventeenth Century. Meeting: Wednesday evenings at 7:30 p.m. in the Church Room.'

'And that's this evening,' said Paul with satisfaction. 'May as well go to our respective homes and get something to eat.'

'He might at least have offered to whip me up an omelette,' grumbled Agatha to her cats as she defrosted a microwave meal and hoped it was something she felt like eating. The frost had been so thick that she could not read the label.

She felt uneasily that they were wasting time going to this historical society. Ten to one, Harry Witherspoon had murdered his mother.

Chapter Five

Agatha Raisin lay in a scented bath and wondered whether it was all worth getting out of it, getting dressed, and going to the Towdey Historical Society. This was not because she was sure Harry was the murderer, but rather because she felt a need to relax – a rare need. Normally Agatha never felt comfortable just slopping around, doing nothing. The fact was she was fed up with herself for always going to endless lengths to prepare herself and dress up for men who were not worth the effort. Paul is married, remember that, she told herself severely.

Her cats, Hodge and Boswell, sat on the edge of the bath and stared at her solemnly as if agreeing with her thoughts.

Hidden treasure and secret passages. It all reminded her of the comics she had read as a child. Still – someone had got into that house . . .

With a sigh, she rose out of the now tepid water and dried herself. She then studied her body in the mirror. Her breasts were still high, and she had no cellulite or stretch marks. But there was a slackening of the skin at the waist, at the stomach, and under her chin. She decided to do some waist exercises the following day. She had always had a thick waistline. No sense in letting it get worse.

She rebelled against the idea of wearing pretty underwear. Why bother when she was going out with a married man? She put on a pair of white cotton knickers and a white cotton bra and then went through to the bedroom and selected a comfortable linen trouser suit and white blouse. Agatha resisted the temptation to put on high heels. She was just making her way downstairs with the cats running in front of her when the doorbell rang. She looked at her watch. Paul was right on time.

'Ready?' he asked when she opened the door. 'You look really nice.'

Well, thought Agatha, you never could tell with men. Maybe one looked more available with the minimum of make-up.

'Do you really think anything will come out of this?' she asked.

'Might do. It's worth a try.'

It was still light as they drove off, but a grey evening with flashes of sheet lightning over to the west and the occasional rumble of thunder. 'Maybe we should have checked out where the church room was before we left Towdey,' said Agatha.

'The church is at the end of the main street and the church room is bound to be next to it.'

'Heard from your wife?'

'Juanita? No. No news is good news. Heard from your ex? Gossip round the village says you're still in love with him.'

'I haven't heard from him and I don't want to,' said Agatha harshly.

They continued on to Towdey in silence.

Paul parked in front of the church. It had a grey Norman tower and the west door had a Norman arch over it. Old gravestones, some of them slanted at crazy angles, stood on the rough grass of the churchyard. A heavy drop of rain struck Agatha's cheek and the thunder rumbled closer.

'Let's find that church room,' cried Agatha. 'It's just about to pour.'

An elderly man and woman walked into the churchyard. 'Are you going to the historical society?' asked Paul. 'We don't know where the church room is.'

'Follow us,' said the old man.

'They're a bit historical themselves,' said Agatha as they slowly followed the couple round the corner of the church and up shallow steps to an open door. There were six more elderly people already seated in a small square room, and three middle-aged punters, fidgeting and yawning.

A tall slim man was arranging some papers on a lectern facing the audience. When he saw Agatha and Paul, he walked forward to meet them. 'I am Peter Frampton,' he said. 'Nice to see two new faces at our little gathering.'

Paul introduced them while Agatha covertly studied Peter Frampton, deciding he was quite attractive in a scholarly way. She put his age somewhere in the early forties. He had beautifully barbered grey hair, all waves and curls. His face was thin with a good straight nose and his pale grey eyes were heavy-lidded.

'There are two seats at the front,' Peter was saying. 'I don't know why it is; but nobody wants to sit at the front.'

'We'll break the pattern, then,' said Paul, ushering Agatha forward.

'Are you interested in the Civil War?' he asked.

'Very,' said Agatha.

'Good, good. Just about to start.'

A great flash of lightning whitened the room and several members of the audience screamed.

'It's just a storm and it will soon pass,' said Peter, taking his place behind the lectern. 'Good evening, ladies and gentlemen. Some of you have told me that you have insufficient knowledge of the Civil War. I think therefore tonight I will concentrate on the Battle of Worcester, 1651, which was the final act in the Civil War, which began in August 1642. Now the Cavaliers were so called from the Spanish caballeros, and the Roundheads because they were considered lowly Puritan artisans, not gentlemen, with

107

cropped heads. The Cavaliers favoured flowing locks. Now to the battle.

'On August 28, part of the Parliamentary Army –'

'Who they?' quavered an old voice.

'The Roundheads.'

'Arr.'

'They crossed the river Severn at Upton. By nightfall –'

The door to the back of the hall opened with a bang. Agatha twisted round to look at the new-comer and then nudged Paul in the ribs. 'Have a look,' she whispered. 'It's life, but not as we know it, Jim.'

A girl stood at the entrance. Behind her in the churchyard, rain drummed down in silver rods. Her thick brown hair was worn on top of her head and held in place with silver combs. Her face was white and her lips purple. She had painted thick black lines around her eyes. She was wearing a sleeveless leather tunic with heavy silver baroque jewellery and tight black leather trousers with knee-high boots which had silver clasps down the side and enormously high heels.

'Come in, Zena, and close the door,' said Peter, looking not in the slightest taken aback by this vision.

The thunder crashed but Peter's voice rose above it. After half an hour, Agatha realized that he was still at the Battle of Worcester and showed no sign of moving on to the Royalist history of Towdey.

By the time he had got to the end of the battle, where the Cavaliers were routed and King Charles had escaped, the thunder was rumbling off into the distance. 'Around ten thousand Scottish prisoners were stripped of their possessions. Some were placed in prisons around the country, others were transported to New England, Virginia and the West Indies to work on the plantations and iron works. Others were sent to work on the drainage schemes on the fens. Many of the English prisoners were conscripted into the army and were sent to Ireland.

'I hope this lecture has gone some way to fill in the gaps in your knowledge. Shall we break for tea, and then I will take your questions.'

A woman rose from the audience and whipped off a white cloth on a trestle-table revealing a tea urn and plates of sandwiches and cakes. Agatha stood up and looked around for Zena but she was nowhere in sight. She must have left more quietly than she had arrived.

'May as well get some tea,' said Paul. The elderly were rapidly piling up their plates with mounds of sandwiches and cakes. 'Are you interested in history?' Paul asked an elderly gentleman. 'Not me,' he said cheerfully. 'Me, I comes for the food.'

'There's not much left,' grumbled Agatha. 'Bloody gannets.'

'Their need is greater than yours,' said Paul.

'How would you like to have to manage on an old age pension?'

'I wonder why that odd-looking girl called Zena decided to show up?'

'Who knows? Maybe checking on her grandmother. She looked dressed for the disco rather than a historical society meeting.'

Paul looked around. 'Peter Frampton has gone missing as well,' he said. 'I hope he'll be back to take questions.'

'There's another door behind that screen at the back of the room,' said Agatha. 'Maybe he went there.'

'Oh, here he is again,' said Paul as Peter emerged from behind the screen.

'While you are enjoying your tea,' he announced, 'are there any questions?' Agatha put up her hand. 'Yes, Mrs Er . . .'

'I thought this was going to be a lecture on the Royalists in Towdey,' said Agatha.

'It was. But several members said they would like to know a bit of the background of the Civil War. Perhaps next week.'

Paul put up his hand. 'Can you tell us a bit about Sir Geoffrey Lamont?'

'In a moment. Mr Bragg had his hand up first. Mr Bragg?'

'Why weren't there none of them fairy cakes this time?'

'Mrs Partlett is on holiday. She usually supplies them. She will be back next week.'

A ferocious discussion on the merits of fairy cakes erupted. Paul put his hand up again.

'Mrs Harper,' said Peter.

Paul glared his annoyance.

'I would like to read out the minutes of the last meeting,' quavered Mrs Harper in a nervous voice.

'My apologies. I forgot. Do proceed.'

Paul sank back in his chair. 'This is getting interesting,' whispered Agatha. 'He's deliberately avoiding answering your question.'

And so it seemed. For the minute Mrs Harper had finished, Peter said, 'Well, that wraps it up. See you all next week.'

Paul rose to his feet but Peter scurried off behind the screen and they heard a door slam.

'That's that,' said Agatha. 'We'll find out where he lives and tackle him at his home.'

'Let's ask some of the locals about Ivy Cottage. Mr Bragg,' said Paul, approaching that elderly gentleman.

'Yuss?'

'Can you tell us anything about the history of Ivy Cottage?'

'Where her was killed?'

'Yes.'

'It be an old place. Tudor.'

'We know that,' said Paul impatiently. 'Weren't there supposed to be jewels hidden there?'

'Oh, that old story. Naw. Nary a one, I reckon. If there was anything, it was stolen long afore

I was born and that weren't yesterday.' He laughed, spraying Paul with cake crumbs.

'We might be interested in buying it,' said Agatha.

'Then you should see Mr Frampton. He were arter it, but the old girl wouldn't budge.'

Agatha's eyes gleamed with excitement. 'Do you know where Mr Frampton lives?'

'Third cottage down from the pub. Faggots Bottom.'

Agatha blinked at him. 'That can't be the name of the place!'

'That it is. Always was. Course Mr Frampton just has a number outside. Didn't hold with the name.'

A watery sunlight was sparkling off raindrops on the old trees surrounding the churchyard when they left.

'So what do you think?' asked Paul when they got into the car.

'It could be a front, the historical society, I mean,' said Agatha, ever eager to discover major crime syndicates in the Cotswold villages.

He laughed. 'No, you weren't paying attention. He gave a very good lecture. He was passionate about it. He doesn't really care if most of the audience only come for the eats.'

'But what about that girl who came in? Totally out of place.'

'She may be a relative. Stop speculating and see if we can get some facts.'

112

They drove slowly past the pub and counted off two cottages and stopped outside the third.

'There's a light on, anyway,' said Agatha. 'Must be at home.'

'Unless he left it on as security.'

They got out of the car and walked to the cottage door. Agatha rang the bell.

The door opened and Peter Frampton surveyed them impatiently. 'Is it important?' he asked.

'We wanted to ask you about Ivy Cottage,' said Agatha.

'Well, what about it?'

'Do you mind if we come in for a moment?' asked Paul.

'Just for a minute,' he said reluctantly.

He turned away and they followed him into a small dark living-room. He did not ask them to sit, simply stood facing them.

'The story of Sir Geoffrey Lamont's jewels,' said Paul. 'Any truth in that story?'

'I believe there is, or rather was. There is a short history of the village published in the nineteenth century. Evidently one of the owners around 1884 practically had the cottage dismantled looking for the treasure, but nothing was found.'

'What about secret passages?'

Peter Frampton threw back his head and laughed. 'None of those. I once got Mrs Witherspoon's permission to search Ivy Cottage, but

113

there was nothing odd there. No jewels, no secret passage.'

'Well, that's that,' said Agatha, disappointed. 'Thank you for your time.'

'So where do we go from here?' asked Agatha as they drove off. 'No wicked hotel owner, no sinister man from the historical society.'

'Someone killed her and it was probably Harry. Let's concentrate on Harry.'

'Not much good. The police will have been concentrating their efforts on Harry and I don't see that we can find out anything they can't. What about the daughter? She may have known she wasn't going to get anything and murdered her mother in a rage.'

'Let's leave it until tomorrow. I'm tired.'

'And I'm hungry,' said Agatha, hoping he would ask her out for dinner.

'I'll leave you to your microwave meals.' Paul laughed and Agatha repressed an impulse to hit him.

Agatha slept heavily and woke to the sounds of cleaning. Doris Simpson, who 'did' for Agatha, had obviously arrived.

Agatha washed and dressed and went downstairs just as Doris emerged from the kitchen. 'Morning, Agatha,' said Doris, who was one of the very few women in the village to use Agatha's first name.

'Come into the kitchen and join me for a coffee, Doris. I want to know if you've heard anything.'

'I made a fresh pot of coffee.' Doris sat down at the kitchen table. 'I let your cats out into the garden.'

'Thanks,' said Agatha. 'How's Scrabble?'

Scrabble was a cat Agatha had rescued during one of her cases. Feeling that three cats were too much, she had given Scrabble to the cleaner.

'Scrabble's blooming,' said Doris. She helped herself to three spoonfuls of sugar and then a generous topping of milk. 'Don't know how you can drink it straight black like that. What do you want to know?'

'Have you heard any gossip about Mrs Witherspoon?'

'That old woman that got murdered? She did get murdered, didn't she? There was a bit in the paper this morning. I didn't see it, but someone in the village told me.'

'Yes, it came out at the inquest. So, heard anything?'

'Too early yet, Agatha. You see, up till this morning, everyone thought it was an accident. But I'll ask around. I hear you've been seeing a lot of your neighbour.' She tilted her head to one side and peered at Agatha through her glasses.

'I've been asking around about Mrs Witherspoon and he's been helping me.'

'Doesn't do to mess with married men.'

115

'I'm not messing with him,' said Agatha crossly. 'And I've met his wife.'

'Oh, that Spanish woman. Very rude, she was. Told one of my ladies that Carsely was a living grave and she wasn't ever coming back.'

'I think she's very temperamental,' said Agatha cautiously. 'She wants her husband to live in Spain.'

'What does he think about that?' asked Doris.

Agatha shrugged. 'Don't believe he wants to, but it's none of my business.'

The doorbell rang. 'I'll get it,' said Agatha.

She opened the front door to Detective Sergeant Bill Wong. 'Official?' asked Agatha.

'Semi,' he said, following her indoors. 'I wondered if you had unearthed anything.'

'Nothing much. Coffee?'

'Yes, please. Morning, Doris.'

'Morning, Bill. I'll get on with my work, Agatha. I was going to feed the cats for you, in case you wanted a long lie-in, but I couldn't find any tins of cat food.'

'I'll get some from the shop this morning.'

When Doris had left and had plugged in the vacuum cleaner and was busily cleaning the living-room, Bill said, 'She doesn't know you feed your cats on fresh fish and pâté, now does she?'

Agatha turned pink. 'I give them a little treat from time to time. So what have you found out?'

'It's hard to pin-point the exact time of death,

116

but from eight that evening until midnight, Harry Witherspoon was in an amateur production of *The Mikado* in Mircester. He's in the chorus. He attended the back-stage party after the show, which went on late.'

'But she was found in her night-gown. It could have happened during the night.'

'From the contents of her stomach, the pathologist suggests she probably died around eleven o'clock.'

'Rats! He never left the theatre?'

'Not according to witnesses. Have you got anything?'

Agatha sighed. 'Nothing. We spent a dreary evening at the historical society at Towdey.'

'Why there?'

'Ivy Cottage is an old house. During the Civil War, a Cavalier, Sir Geoffrey Lamont, fleeing the Battle of Worcester, took refuge there. He was supposed to be carrying a fortune in jewels and gold with him. His host, Simon Lovesey, unknown, I suppose, to Lamont, was a Cromwell sympathizer and turned him in. Nothing was ever heard of the fortune. Legend has it that the fortune is somewhere in the house.'

'Sounds like a *Boy's Own* story. Hidden treasure!' scoffed Bill. 'Anyway, Simon Lovesey probably became richer or gave the booty to Cromwell.'

'I suppose,' said Agatha. 'Dead ends all round. But the fact remains that even before her death,

117

someone was able to get into the house. There may even be a secret passage.'

'Agatha! I am sure generations of owners have turned the place upside down looking for the jewels. So if there was a secret passage, they'd have found it.'

'Maybe. But would they talk about it? I mean, if they were looking for jewels and only found an old secret passage, would they bother talking about it?'

'You're clutching at straws,' said Bill.

'You haven't even got a straw to clutch at,' commented Agatha, lighting a cigarette. 'Nothing from forensics? No footprints anywhere?'

'Nothing of use.'

'What about the daughter, Carol? She needs money. She might have thought she was inheriting something, or maybe she knew she wasn't and killed her mother in a fit of rage, and she has a key.'

'She's a sad creature and has been treated badly by her mother but she doesn't seem the type to plan such a murder. Whoever did this was cold and calculating. Don't worry. They're working on it.'

'They? Not you?'

'No, the case is being handled by Detective Inspector Runcorn.'

'Oh, him! Nasty chauvinist.'

'Agatha, it's no use trying to talk like an old-fashioned women's libber when you fall for any man who crosses your path.'

'I do not! I have not fallen for Paul!'

The doorbell rang. 'I'll get it,' called Doris.

'It's Mr Chatterton,' she called.

Bill grinned as Agatha squawked and ran for the stairs. 'Tell him I'll be down in a minute.'

When Agatha came back to join them, Bill noticed the pretty summer dress and the newly applied make-up.

'It's seems no one's getting anywhere,' said Paul. He turned to Bill. 'Will you be at the funeral tomorrow?'

'Not my case. I've no doubt Runcorn, who's in charge of it, will be there.' Paul flashed a warning look at Agatha. How could they steal the house key and not be observed?

'I'd better get on,' said Bill. 'If I hear anything interesting I'll let you know.'

'That's odd,' said Agatha after he had left.

'What's odd?'

'Usually he warns me to stay clear and leave it to the police.'

'Then take it as a compliment to your detective abilities.'

'My detective abilities are not doing much for me in this case.'

'What can we get that the police can't?' said Paul. 'I'll tell you. Gossip. I think we should drive over and see the neighbours again.'

'You mean Greta and Percy?'

'Yes, them.'

'Worth a try, I suppose.' She raised her voice. 'I'm going out for a little, Doris.'

119

'Don't forget to get food for the cats.'

'I won't. Come on, Paul.'

As they drove into Hebberdon, Agatha said, 'We should remember that Greta threatened to stick a bread knife into Mrs Witherspoon.'

'You've met Mrs Witherspoon. Seems just the sort of thing a lot of people must have said to her. But saying and doing are two different things. Oh, look at the roses!' He pointed to where rambling roses in pink and white tumbled over the doorways of two cottages. 'It's almost as if God is compensating us for the dreadful autumn, winter and spring of rain and more rain.'

Agatha grunted. She always felt uneasy when people mentioned the God word. But she had to admit to herself that she became so used to the beauty of the Cotswolds that she was apt to take it all for granted – except two days after a visit to London.

'Well, here's Pear Cottage. Let's start off with Greta.'

Greta answered the door to them, wearing trousers and a sleeveless shirt. Agatha was struck anew at how muscular Greta was. Although small and round, there seemed to be no spare fat on her figure.

'Oh, it's you again,' she said. 'So it's murder. Not surprised. Could have murdered the old bird myself. Come in.'

They followed her into her living-room and sat down.

'The police seem to think that her son Harry did it,' said Paul.

'That little pussy-cat! Know why he kept away from her? She terrified him. Old folks round here say she beat him when he was a boy. That's why he turned out the way he is.'

'What way?' asked Agatha.

'Well, he's a poof, isn't he?'

'Do you mean he is homosexual?' said Agatha.

'Stands to reason. Not married.'

Agatha suddenly thought of James, who had remained a bachelor until his middle age, when he had married her.

'The fact that he is not married,' said Agatha in a cold voice, 'does not mean that he is homosexual. Furthermore, if he is, it does not mean that he is lacking in either brains or courage.'

Greta snorted with contempt. 'You're one of those bleeding-heart liberals.'

Paul suppressed a grin. He wondered if Agatha had ever been accused of such a thing before. But seeing that Agatha was about to renew the attack, he said quickly, 'Did you happen to hear any stories about a secret passage to Ivy Cottage?'

'Not that I 'member. Why?'

'Someone was trying to frighten her. I mean, we spent the night there and there was carbon dioxide gas coming under the door.'

121

'Did that herself to get the attention.'

'Maybe,' said Paul. 'On the other hand, if someone else was doing it, there may be a secret way in. And what about this old story about treasure being hidden in the house?'

'That's all it is. Just an old story.'

'On the night she was killed,' Agatha put in, masking her dislike for Greta, 'you didn't see or hear anyone around? Any strangers reported in the village?'

'You should leave detecting to the police. Don't you think they've asked around? They've had men going from door to door.'

Agatha had had enough. She stood up. 'Thank you for your time. Come along, Paul.'

Paul meekly followed her out.

'Bitch!' said Agatha loudly.

'Shut up. She'll hear you and we might need her again.'

'Heaven forbid,' said Agatha. 'Anyway, I've got a good idea.'

'Like what?'

'Like Harry is now prime suspect, alibi or not. I bet the police still think he might have sneaked over to Hebberdon when no one was looking.'

'What? Dressed as a citizen of Titipu?'

'Say the show finished at ten. He'd still have time to get his make-up off and drive over and then nip back again in time for the party.'

'What's all this about, Agatha?'

'He might be glad of our help. If he wanted our help, he might let us search the house.'

'Long shot.'

'Maybe. But I'll ask him at the funeral tomorrow.'

'I think your timing's wrong.'

'Why? He must have hated his mother after the way she brought him up.'

'Not necessarily. Mothers are mothers.'

'And by all accounts, this one was a right mother, as they say in New York.'

'Tut, Agatha. Shouldn't speak ill of the dead.'

'Why not? I'm just joining the legions who haven't a good word to say for the old bat. Let's see if Percy is in his shed.'

Percy Fleming was delighted to see them. 'A real-live murder and practically on one's doorstep,' he said cheerfully. 'Are you sleuthing? The police have been round but I couldn't really tell them anything.'

'We were wondering whether you knew of any hidden passage in Ivy Cottage,' said Paul.

'I've heard about the treasure but never a word about a secret passage.'

'And you didn't hear or see anything or anyone around on the night of the murder?'

'Not a thing. But I have a Theory.'

'That being?' asked Agatha.

'The daughter did it. Yes, she found the body. But what was she doing on the night of the murder? I asked one of the coppers. He said she was home all evening. Neighbours say her lights were on and heard her television going on until late. But I say, what's to stop her from leaving the lights on and the telly on and nipping over to Hebberdon?'

'I didn't see a car,' said Agatha. 'How did she normally get over here?'

His face fell. 'She took the bus, which arrives here in the morning, stayed with her mother and then took it back again at two in the afternoon.'

'But the buses don't run in the evening, do they?'

'No. But she could have hired a car.'

'So she could,' said Agatha, suddenly weary. It was hot inside the shed and Percy was wearing a very strong aftershave. 'Well, thanks for your help.'

'Waste of space,' grumbled Agatha as they walked back to the car. 'What now?'

'Nothing till the funeral tomorrow.'

Chapter Six

A light drizzle was smearing the window-panes when Agatha woke up the next morning. She struggled out of bed and began to rummage through her wardrobe to find something suitable to wear for the funeral. Church of England meant all black was not necessary, but bright colours might be regarded as offensive. Then she had to wear suitable gear for any nimble action, such as stealing the key and rushing off to get it copied. She opted finally for a dark brown silk trouser suit and a white blouse. She could wear heels with it but carry flat shoes with her in a bag.

She peered anxiously at her hair. A line of grey was showing at the roots. Agatha let out a squawk of dismay. A picture of Juanita with her long black hair rose unbidden in her mind.

She went into the bathroom and rummaged along a shelf of hair conditioners, shampoos and dyes. Forgetting that she had found in the past that to colour her own hair instead of going to the hairdresser was often a mistake, she found a packet of brunette colour shampoo rinse and began to apply it.

Agatha was just reaching for the hairdrier when the doorbell rang. She looked at her watch and found the time was ten-thirty. Must be Paul. Rats! She wrapped a towel around her head and put a dressing-gown on over her underwear and ran down and opened the door.

'Won't be a minute,' she said to Paul.

'You look like more than a minute. Hurry up.'

Agatha ran back upstairs and dried her hair and brushed it into a smooth bob, scrambled into the trouser suit and blouse and surveyed herself in the mirror. The rain had stopped and a watery shaft of sunlight shone in and lit up her hair. She now had red roots.

'Agatha!' shouted Paul impatiently from the bottom of the stairs. Agatha seized a brown suede hat with a floppy brim, jammed it on her head and ran downstairs.

'You look like an agitated mushroom,' commented Paul. 'I assume you're somewhere under that hat. Let's go.'

As he drove them towards Towdey, he glanced sideways at her. 'The sun's out and it's quite warm. Women don't really need to wear hats to funerals any more.'

'I like this hat,' said Agatha truculently. 'It's the height of fashion.'

'Could have fooled me.'

'Are you always this rude?'

'No, but you're a good teacher.'

126

They both relapsed into silence until they reached the church.

Paul parked beside the church wall and they got out and walked through the graveyard. 'Don't suppose she'll be buried here,' said Paul, looking around.

'Why?'

'No room left. Have you noticed when any-one's buried on television it's usually in some old English churchyard? Doesn't happen these days. The places are fairly walled up with the English dead.'

A mischievous breeze danced across the churchyard and whipped Agatha's hat from her head and sent it flying. 'I'll get it,' said Paul and set off in pursuit. He returned with a sodden hat. 'You can't wear it. It ended up in a puddle.' He looked at her hair. 'Quite fetching, you know. Brown hair with red roots.'

Agatha angrily took the wet hat from him and placed it on top of a gravestone.

'There's Runcorn just going into the church,' hissed Paul.

'And Carol,' said Agatha in surprise. 'She looks quite smart and cheerful. Let's see who else has turned up.'

They entered the gloom of the church. It was quite full. Agatha saw Greta Handy and Percy Fleming sitting side by side. She assumed the rest were curious villagers.

'Peter Frampton has just come in with that peculiar girl, Zena,' whispered Paul.

Agatha and Paul had selected a pew at the back of the small church so that they would have a good view of everyone present. Peter walked up the aisle with Zena on his arm. She was wearing a dull red dress of Indian cotton and long wooden beads with clumpy boots. Her hair was worn down and brushed straight and nearly reached to her bottom. She turned her head and looked back down the church. Her make-up was brown with purple eye-shadow and purple lips.

'Odd couple,' murmured Agatha. 'Could be his daughter.'

'Doubt it,' said Paul. 'Hey, what if there isn't any reception?'

'Drive to Ivy Cottage afterwards and hope there is.'

'I wonder whether they still begin with "Dearly Beloved, we are gathered here together . . ." and so on. Probably not. I hate these modern translations of the Bible. They lack the beauty of language in the King James's Version and the absolute faith that underlies the words.'

Solemn music from the organ sounded out in the church. The coffin was carried in. Harry was one of the pallbearers. The others looked as if they had been supplied by the undertaker.

The service began. It was simple and dignified. The vicar gave a short sermon. Old-fashioned hymns were sung. No one read a eulogy. There was no one evidently hypocritical enough to praise the dear departed.

128

Everyone stood while the coffin was carried out and loaded into a hearse.

Agatha and Paul followed the congregation out to the church door, where Harry and Carol stood side by side.

Agatha nervously expected an outburst but Harry said, 'Thank you for coming. Carol and I would appreciate it if you would join us at Ivy Cottage for some refreshments. We would like a word in private with you.'

'Do we go to the graveside first?' asked Agatha.

'No, Mother is being cremated. The funeral people see to that.'

'This sounds hopeful,' said Agatha as they walked back to the car.

'Could be. Or maybe they just wanted to warn us off. Don't you want your hat?'

'Leave it,' said Agatha. 'Did you notice how *friendly* Carol and Harry seemed?'

'Could be an act,' said Paul.

'But Carol was looking almost *happy*. And smartly dressed.'

'Well, we'll find out what it is they want to talk to us about.'

'If they're friendly,' said Agatha, 'we can just ask for permission to search the house.'

'Better not leave it to chance.'

They waited in the car until all the guests and finally Carol and Harry had left and then drove to Ivy Cottage.

The refreshments consisted of sherry and

sandwiches. Agatha eyed them hungrily. But Paul whispered, 'Get the key.'

'Then give me your car keys. I'll need to find a key-cutting place. There's one in Moreton.'

'Or there's the cobbler in Blockley,' said Paul. 'That would be quicker.'

Why they had imagined the key would simply be there, dangling in the lock, was beyond Agatha. Furthermore, there were four locks on the front door. She went through to the kitchen in the back premises but found two women cutting sandwiches and arranging them on plates and retreated.

Paul looked at her in surprise when she rejoined him. 'That was quick.'

'I haven't been anywhere,' said Agatha crossly. 'We should have realized they wouldn't just leave the keys in the door and the front door has four locks.'

'We'll need to rely on their goodwill. Have a sandwich and I'll see if there's a simpler way in from the back.'

'I tried that. There's women in the kitchen.'

'Nonetheless, I'll look around.'

Paul left and Agatha was joined by Percy Fleming. 'I'm surprised to see you here,' said Agatha.

'I like attending funerals,' he fluted. 'I bring the sombre note and ritual into my books.'

'I don't see Peter Frampton here,' said Agatha, looking around.

'Oh, the historical-society man. He goes to

events in Towdey Church because he's from Towdey.'

'Who's that girl with him, Zena something?'

'Zena Saxon. She just appeared, so to speak. Wonderful wardrobe, don't you think? Today's outfit was pure sixties commune.'

'But where's she *from*?'

'She's got a cottage in Towdey, left to her last year by an aunt. Where she was before, I don't know. She and Peter are an item. Quite shocking, considering the age difference.'

'He's a handsome fellow.'

'But Stagey-looking, don't you think?' Percy often seemed to put capital letters on some of his words. 'Quite obsessed with the seventeenth century. Oh, here's that dreary copper.' He moved away and his place was taken by Detective Inspector Runcorn.

'I hope you're not doing anything to interfere with our investigations,' he said.

'Simply paying our respects.'

'A word of warning to you, Mrs Raisin. It's only in books that old biddies from villages can help the police. In real life, they're a pain in the arse.'

'Just like you,' said Agatha savagely. 'Sod off.'

'I'm warning you.'

Agatha turned and walked away. She went up to Carol, who had just said goodbye to Greta Handy, and whispered, 'You wanted to see us?'

'Could you wait a moment? The others will be leaving soon.'

But it was an hour before everyone left and Agatha was just thinking she would have to deal with Harry and Carol on her own when Paul reappeared.

'Right,' said Harry after he had said goodbye to the last guest. 'Please sit down.'

Agatha, tired of standing, sank gratefully into an armchair.

'It's like this,' said Harry. 'Although I have an alibi, the police still suspect me. Neither Carol nor I can get any money until we're totally cleared.'

'I thought Carol didn't inherit anything.'

Carol threw her brother a radiant smile. 'Dear Harry's arranged with the lawyers that I get half of everything. We got talking, you see, and found out how Mother had deliberately turned us against each other.'

'If you do get the money,' said Agatha, looking at Harry, 'will you keep on your business?'

'No, I'll sell it. I was pretty successful until the last two years. Rising business rates and falling sales have crippled me. I spent too much money at auctions buying antiques that no one seems to want.'

'So what did you want to see us about?' asked Paul.

'The police aren't trying hard enough because they think it's me or Carol. I remember reading about you, Mrs Raisin. So we want you to find out who killed Mother. When we get the money, we'll pay you for your trouble.'

'Oh, that's all right,' said Agatha with the airy

unconcern of the new rich, 'we've been investigating anyway. What we did wonder is if you could let us explore the house. You see, whoever was trying to frighten your mother must have found a way of getting in here. Might be a secret passage or something like that.'

'Perhaps later,' said Harry, after a glance at his sister. 'We need to finish up here.'

'Then if we borrowed the keys from you, we could come back when no one's around,' said Paul.

'I don't think you need to do that,' said Carol. 'I mean, the question is, who murdered her?'

'But don't you see,' said Agatha, exasperated, 'if it wasn't you or Harry, then someone else must have had a way of getting inside the house.'

Harry rose to his feet. 'Carol and I are feeling a bit shaky after the funeral. Can we leave things for the moment?' And without waiting for a reply, he walked across the room and held the door open for them.

'Well!' exclaimed Agatha as they got in the car. 'What did you make of that?'

'Very odd,' said Paul. 'I mean, they want us to find the murderer and then they both stick their heels in at the very idea we might want to search the house. Never mind, I've got a key.'

'You have! How? Where from?'

'There are two doors out to the back. One from

the kitchen, which has several locks and bolts, but there is one from a scullery. It's a dusty old door and I don't think it's been used for years. But it had a key in the lock. I slid it out. I told the women working in the kitchen that I'd dropped my notebook when we were ghost-hunting, which gave me an excuse to search around. Once I'd got the key, I broke the speed limit to Moreton and got it copied. So let's try tonight.'

'Pity we'll need to crawl around with pencil torches.'

'I've been thinking about that. Neither Carol nor Harry lives near here. Unless you were actually walking past the house, you wouldn't be able to see any lights. We'll switch them on and start our search. If anyone does happen to be, say, walking their dog in the middle of the night and gets suspicious, they'll ring the bell at the front and we can beat a retreat from the back.'

Agatha was suddenly mesmerized by his arm nearest her on the wheel. He had slung his jacket in the back of the car before driving off. It was a tanned and muscular arm. She felt a strong sexual frisson and then she remembered Juanita. Forget him. Maybe somewhere out there was an unmarried man, charming and kind and intelligent, who would be prepared to throw in his lot with Agatha Raisin for life.

Agatha had not considered black de rigueur for

a funeral but decided it was necessary for house-breaking. The evening was warm and humid but she did not have a black blouse and settled for a thin black sweater worn with black trousers and flat black shoes. Paul was to call for her at two o'clock. Just before he came, she decided that she might as well play the part properly, and putting her hand up the living-room chimney, she collected a handful of soot and blacked her face.

Paul, calling for her at exactly two o'clock, reeled back when he saw her and said faintly, 'Trick or treat.'

'It's no use us wearing black with our faces shining white,' said Agatha defiantly.

'Oh, go and wash it off. If anyone should be up and sees you in the car looking like that, they'll be gossiping about it in the morning all over Carsely.'

But after Agatha had scrubbed off the soot and put on make-up and they were driving through Carsely, Mrs Davenport looked down from her bedroom window and saw them. Her lips tightened in disapproval. Mr Chatterton's wife should know what he was up to with that harpy. They probably thought they were avoiding gossip by driving off to some hotel for their assignation. But the wife was in Madrid. I wonder if Mrs Bloxby has Mrs Chatterton's home address, mused Mrs Davenport.

As before, they parked outside the village and

then walked towards Bag End and so to Ivy Cottage.

It stood, dark and sinister, in the moonlight. A light breeze sent the ivy rustling and whispering. Agatha looked at the house uneasily. 'You don't think it really is haunted?' she asked.

'Nonsense. Let's go round the back.'

He unlatched a gate at the side of the house. The hinges sent out a creaking noise which sounded eerily loud in the silence of the night.

Agatha suddenly wished she were home in bed with her cats for company. She felt small and lonely and isolated. She wondered what Paul thought of her.

'Right,' said Paul, switching on a pencil torch. 'Here's the back, and the scullery door should be along here next to the kitchen one.' Agatha followed the dancing beam of the torch until it lighted on the scullery door.

'I don't like this,' she whispered. 'I don't think this is a good idea.'

'Shhh!' He took a key out of his pocket and inserted it in the lock. 'Very hard to turn,' he muttered. 'I should have brought some oil.' He gave a wrench and the key turned with a rasping sound.

Paul moved quietly into the scullery followed by Agatha, who closed the door behind them.

'I think the first thing we do is look for a cellar,' he said. 'Good place to start.'

They walked through the kitchen and into a stone-flagged passage which led to the front of the house. 'This might be it,' said Paul, stopping before a low door. 'Thank goodness the key's in the lock.'

He opened the door and shone the torch around inside until he located a light switch. The dim light of a forty-watt bulb lit up a flight of steep stone steps.

'Down we go,' said Paul cheerfully.

Agatha followed him slowly, always listening for the wail of an approaching police siren.

Paul found another light switch at the bottom of the steps. Agatha joined him and they stood shoulder to shoulder surveying the cellar. It was crammed with old trunks and boxes. 'It'll take us years to get through this lot,' mourned Agatha.

'We're looking for a hidden passage, remember?'

Agatha sighed. 'I'll search along two walls and you take the other two.'

'I wonder . . .'

'What?' demanded Agatha impatiently, anxious for the search to be over.

'If someone got in from outside, it might have been by way of a tunnel from the garden.'

'But there's a huge acreage out there!'

'I mean, there might be some sort of trapdoor on the floor.'

'If there was, Mrs Witherspoon would have found it.'

'Not necessarily,' said Paul. 'A lot of this junk must have come with the house. Look at the name on this trunk, "Joseph Henderson".' He bent down and rummaged in a box. 'There are schoolbooks here dated 1902! I think she just left all this stuff untouched.'

'But you would think Harry and Carol would have come down here when they were children.'

'Might have forbidden them to do so.' Paul moved over to another section of the cellar, searching in boxes. 'No, here we have Harry's schoolbooks and some dolls which must have belonged to Carol.'

'The floor's dusty,' said Agatha, suddenly interested. 'Look around and see if any of the boxes have been moved.' She backed into an old rocking horse and let out a squeak of alarm as the horse dipped backwards and forwards as if it still had a child on its back.

An hour passed as they searched and searched. 'Hopeless,' said Agatha, sitting down on a trunk. Her arms ached from moving piles of stuff around. Paul came and sat down next to her.

'We've moved everything and looked underneath,' he sighed.

'Except that wooden chest over there,' said Agatha. 'Too heavy. I couldn't budge it.'

'What's in it?'

'I didn't look.'

'Agatha!'

'Well, I'm tired and I'm frightened we'll get caught.'

'Wait till I look in the chest. Where is it?'

'Under that pile of old curtains. I put everything back the way it was.'

Agatha fumbled in her pocket and took out a packet of cigarettes and a lighter. Paul, who was heading in the direction of the chest, turned round. 'No cigarettes, Agatha. The smell of smoke will linger.'

Agatha sulkily put her cigarettes back in her pocket and stifled a yawn.

Paul heaved aside the curtains, which sent up a cloud of dust, making him sneeze. He opened the lid of the large chest. 'More curtains,' he said, lifting them out.

'Anything underneath?' asked Agatha.

'Nothing. Wait a bit. There are scratch marks on the edge of the wood at the bottom.'

'So what?' demanded Agatha, craving a cigarette.

Paul fished in his pocket and drew out a knife. His head disappeared inside the chest. 'The bottom comes up. You can prise it up,' he said.

Agatha, suddenly excited, went to join him.

Paul struggled and strained and lifted out the bottom of the chest. 'Look at that,' he said, straightenlng up.

Revealed was a trapdoor in the floor, and on top of the trapdoor was what looked like a new ring fastened to it.

He heaved on the ring. The trapdoor eased up and then fell against the side of the chest with a crash. Paul swore and they both waited in silence. 'It's all right,' said Paul with a shaky laugh. 'I doubt if anything can be heard from this cellar. I'm going down. Look at those wooden steps, some of them look new, as if recently repaired.'

He made his way down, shining his torch, and Agatha followed him. They found themselves in a stone passage. The air was dry and musty and the ceiling so low, they had to half-crouch to walk along it.

'What if the air is so bad that we'll die?' said Agatha, hanging on to the end of his sweater as she followed him.

'I forgot the canary,' he joked. 'The air's okay. In fact, it's getting a little bit fresher. Maybe we're near the end.'

They went along in silence. 'Dead end,' said Paul. 'But more steps. I'll go up first. There's bound to be another trapdoor.'

He mounted the steps. Agatha waited anxiously. She heard him grunt as he strained to lift something. Then there was a thud. 'Come on up,' whispered Paul. 'We've come out somewhere.'

Agatha began to climb and then squawked as twigs and leaves fell down on her. 'Sorry,' called Paul. 'I'm trying to move stuff away. It was covering the trapdoor.'

Agatha emerged into the gloom of a thicket. 'If we crouch down, we can get out of here without tearing our clothes,' said Paul. 'There's a sort of tunnel through the bushes.'

Agatha followed the beam of his torch. Outside the thicket, they found themselves quite a way away from the house in a remote part of the garden which looked as if it had never been tended. Thick grass and bushes grew all around.

'Now we know how someone got in,' said Paul.

'Let's get out of here.' Agatha looked around uneasily. 'I'm beginning to get the creeps.'

'All right. Down the ladder with you and I'll replace the trapdoor and try to get as much of the camouflage back on the outside of the lid before I do. Don't want anyone to know we've been here.'

Agatha waited at the bottom of the stairs until Paul closed the trapdoor and joined her with the torch.

With Paul leading the way, Agatha followed him at a half-crouch to avoid bumping her head on the roof. But halfway along the passage, he came to an abrupt stop. 'What is it?' hissed Agatha.

'There's an alcove here, a niche. Sort of thing you get in railway tunnels for the workmen to back into when a train is coming.' He shone the torch in. 'Nothing here.' He shone the torch upwards. 'I think this is a sort of chimney, like an old ventilator. But it's now got blocked at the top. If you stand on my clasped hands, Agatha, and I heave you up, you could feel around and see if anything's been hidden up there.'

'Oh, all right,' muttered Agatha. 'But I won't feel safe until I get out of here.'

Paul heaved her up. Agatha thrust up her hands and dislodged dry leaves and rubble. A stone hit Paul on the face and he lost his hold on Agatha just as her hand located a piece of iron sticking out of the inside on the alcove. She hung on desperately, but the iron spike or whatever it was began to give. She tumbled down on to Paul and they both fell on to the floor as more stones and leaves clattered down on them.

'You're a heavy woman,' grumbled Paul, pushing her off him. 'I've dropped the torch and the damn thing has gone out. Help me feel around for it.'

On their hands and knees they groped around, until Paul cried, 'I've got it,' and at the same time, Agatha said, 'There's a packet or something or other here. Must have fallen down. Shine the torch.'

'I'll see if it's still working. Good, it is. What have you got there?'

The thin beam of the torch shone on a dusty leather-wrapped package. 'Must have fallen out of somewhere,' said Agatha. 'Let's take it with us. I don't want to spend any more time in this house. Not the jewels, anyway. Feels like some sort of book.'

She felt relieved when they were finally up the stairs to the cellar and then up and out of the cellar and out of the house. They hurried to the car.

'I hope no one saw us,' panted Agatha when she finally sank into the car seat. 'Now, what do we do? We should tell the police about that passage. That's how someone got into the house to frighten her.'

'We can't tell them,' said Paul. 'They'd want to know how we found it. Let's get back to your place and have a look at what we've found.'

Once back in Agatha's cottage, she placed the leather package reverently on the kitchen table. Paul carefully unwrapped it, revealing a leather-bound book. He opened it. 'It's a diary!' he said. 'It's Lamont's diary.'

'Does it say anything about his treasure?' asked Agatha.

'Let's see. It's a detailed account of the preparations for the Battle of Worcester and an inventory of provisions and arms.' He turned the pages. 'Then there's a description of the battle.'

'Skip to the end,' said Agatha excitedly. 'He'd hide the treasure when he knew the battle was lost.'

'Don't rush me!'

Paul turned the pages to the end of the book with what seemed to Agatha maddening slowness.

'Here we are,' said Paul. 'He must have written this last bit when he took refuge with Simon Lovesey. "Such Gold and Jewels as I had with me, I buried in Timmin's Field, north of Worcester, before making my Circuitous Way to Hebberdon to seek Refuge. I have not told Mine Host this although he pressures me for Information in an odd way. I shall hide this record until I am sure that his Sympathy with Our Cause is safe."'

Paul closed the book, his eyes shining with excitement. 'So now we know where the treasure is.'

'Let's go and look for it tomorrow,' cried Agatha. 'If we find anything, we can see if Lamont's got any remaining descendants alive.'

'Timmin's Field,' mused Paul. 'Timmin was probably a farmer.'

'I've got an Ordnance Survey map of the Worcester area,' said Agatha. She hurried off and came back with the map. But although they searched the names of all the farms to the north of Worcester, they could not find the name Timmin.

'The farm could have been sold to other people ages ago,' said Paul. 'We need some seventeenth-century maps.'

'We'll go to the records office in Worcester tomorrow,' said Agatha. 'We'd better get some sleep.'

She saw him to the door. 'You're a Trojan, Agatha,' said Paul, smiling down at her. 'This is the most exciting thing that ever happened to me!'

He flung his arms round her and bent and kissed her on the lips.

144

Agatha blinked up at him in a dazed way.

'Goodnight,' he said gently. 'See you at ten in the morning. Get a good sleep.'

Agatha carefully shut the door behind him and then danced up the stairs to bed, her heart racing. He would divorce Juanita and marry her! James Lacey would see the announcement of their wedding and she hoped like hell he suffered!

Murder was forgotten as the excited pair set out for Worcester in the morning. The sun shone down on the Vale of Evesham, stretching all the way to the Malvern Hills. Agatha was driving. She was in control. She had a handsome man beside her who had kissed her last night and she was off on a treasure hunt.

The first cloud appeared on the horizon of her mind when she parked outside the records office and Paul said cautiously, 'Worcester's a very big place. Must have been relatively small by comparison in the seventeenth century.'

'Don't be a downer,' said Agatha. 'Timmin's Field, here we come.'

Inside the records office, they asked for maps of Worcester for the period covering the mid-seventeenth century.

'Rats!' said Agatha as they both bent over it. 'Worcester *is* small.'

'Let's see. North,' said Paul. 'Look north.'

His long finger moved to the north of the city.

'There it is!' he cried. 'Timmin's Field. Timmin must have been a tenant farmer. It's part of the Burnhaddomm estate.'

'Let's go,' said Agatha, beside herself with excitement. 'We should buy a metal detector first. We –'

'Agatha,' said Paul, 'I think we should look at a present-day map of Worcester. That field might be covered over by now.'

'Oh, I've brought the map with me.' Agatha fished it out of her capacious handbag.

They opened it up and compared it with the seventeenth-century one.

'It's been built over. It's a shopping mall. And houses for miles around as well.'

'We'll go and look anyway,' said Agatha, determined. 'Timmin's Field might be a car park now or something that could be dug up.'

'But Worcester continued to spread out since 1651,' said Paul. 'I think we should look at eighteenth- and nineteenth-century maps first.'

'Why?'

'Think, Agatha. Any building on that field means the ground would be dug up. Deep digging to make cellars for houses. The treasure would be found, and believe me, whoever found it would keep quiet about it.'

They got the eighteenth- and nineteenth-century maps and pored over them. 'Look here,' said Paul. 'The nineteenth-century one. Rows and rows of houses right over where Timmin's Field was, and even a church.'

'That can't be right. They wouldn't bulldoze a church!'

Paul got to his feet and returned with a map of Worcester dated 1945. 'There's your answer,' he said. 'That area was bombed during the war. Let's return all these maps.'

Outside, Agatha said stubbornly, 'I still want to see it.'

'As you wish, but it's hopeless. You drive, I'll direct you.'

Agatha finally pulled up outside a giant shopping mall. 'How big would you say Timmin's Field was?' she asked.

'Six acres, I guess.'

'Well, that monstrosity is over six acres. You're right. With all that building and digging, the treasure's long gone.'

'And we're left with a valuable record of the Civil War and we can't tell anyone how we got it,' said Paul. 'Let's have something to eat and decide what to do next.'

'I want comfort food, junk food,' said Agatha.

'Then turn around and go back a bit. I saw one of those all-day breakfast places.'

Agatha, having demolished a plate of egg, sausage, bacon and chips, sat back in her chair with a sigh. 'Now, I can think. First of all, we'll need to figure out what to do with that book of Lamont's.'

'I only glanced through it. It's closely written

147

and full of detail, as far as I could judge. We'll need to find out if there are any descendants of Sir Geoffrey Lamont, and if we find even one, just post the book to them anonymously.'

'There's something that is really worrying,' said Agatha.

'What's that?'

'The secret passage. You noticed that the stairs had been repaired. I think Harry and Carol knew about the passage. They certainly didn't want us to look for it. We can't tell the police or we'll need to explain what we were doing in the house. Even if we found a way of tipping Bill off and the forensic team got down there, they'd find our fingerprints all over the place. We didn't wear gloves.'

'If either Harry or Carol knew about it, why would they want us to find the murderer for them? I mean, if one or both of them murdered their mother?'

Agatha scowled horribly. Then her face cleared. 'What if,' she said, 'just what if neither of them committed murder at all, but had been using the passage to try to frighten their mother to death?'

Paul shook his head. 'Won't do. They both knew their mother would not be easily frightened.'

'Wait a minute! I've just thought of something. Why was Harry offering her house for sale to that hotel chain *before* she died?'

'I think we'd better go and ask him, don't you?'

They called at the shop first but it was Saturday afternoon and there was a CLOSED sign on the door.

'Funny, that,' said Agatha. 'A lot of tourists come to Mircester. You would think he'd stay open on Saturdays.'

'Better try his home,' said Paul.

At that moment, Mrs Bloxby was studying Mrs Davenport. 'You say you want Mrs Chatterton's address in Madrid? Why don't you ask Mr Chatterton?'

'I would do,' said Mrs Davenport crossly, 'if he were ever at home, but he's always out with that Raisin woman. Disgraceful, I call it, a woman of her years, and with a married man, too.'

In an even voice, the vicar's wife said, 'Mrs Raisin and Mr Chatterton are of the same age. They are investigating this murder. That is all. I hope you will keep this in mind and not go around the village spreading malicious gossip.'

Thwarted, Mrs Davenport left the vicarage. How could she get that address? Who else might have it? Then she thought of Miss Simms, the secretary of the ladies' society. She had a list of addresses. Juanita had attended one meeting. Perhaps Miss Simms had taken a note of the address. She headed for the council house estate. She could not understand why such a respectable body as the ladies' society should have a secretary who was an unmarried mother and lived on a council estate. Definitely Not One of Us, thought Mrs Davenport grimly as she walked up the neat garden path leading to Miss Simms's home and rang the bell.

'Oh, it's you,' said Miss Simms. 'I'm just going out.'

'I wondered if you had Mrs Chatterton's address in Madrid.'

'I dunno. I'll have a look. Come in. Hey, wait a bit. Why not ask her husband?'

'He is never at home.'

'Then just shove a note through his door.'

Mrs Davenport's bosom swelled. 'Be a good little girl and see if you can get me that address. Chop-chop.'

'Shan't.'

'I *beg* your pardon?' declared Mrs Davenport in the tones of Edith Evans saying, 'In a *handbag*?'

'I said I won't give it to you, so shove off, you old trout. I've got a feeling you're out to make trouble.'

'Well, really!'

Mrs Davenport stormed off.

She's out to make life hell for our Mrs Raisin, thought Miss Simms. Better warn her.

But at that moment the doorbell rang again and it was Miss Simms's new gentleman friend who travelled in soft furnishings, and somehow the whole scene with Mrs Davenport was forgotten.

Harry opened the door of his home to Agatha and Paul. 'It's you,' he said. 'Find out anything?'

'Not yet, but we want to ask you something.'

'Come in.'

He turned round to face them. 'What is it?'

'Why did you try to sell your mother's house to a hotel chain before she was murdered?'

He had been scowling, but his face cleared. 'Oh, that's easy. My business was failing and I wanted to see if Mother would bail me out. She told me, calm as anything, that she had invested unwisely and she had no spare cash. I pointed out that the house was too big for one person. She could sell it, move into sheltered accommodation and live off the interest on the money she could bank from the sale of the house.

'Mother said she wouldn't get enough to make her want to move. I said I would prove to her how much she would get. I approached the hotel company. At first they were interested, but then they found that to make the necessary alterations would need planning permission and they were pretty sure they wouldn't get it. Mother seemed delighted at my failure. But then, she always loved me to fail,' he added bitterly.

'Have you thought of any enemies she might have had?' asked Paul.

'She must have made scores. She delighted in making people's lives a misery. There's Barry Briar, for one.'

'The landlord?'

'Yes, him. Mother was teetotal and disapproved of drinking. She was always trying to find ways to get him closed down. Then she was always rowing with people in the village.'

'And you don't know of any secret passage into the house?'

'There is no secret passage. I would have known about it.'

'What about Peter Frampton?'

'Who's he?'

'He runs a historical society in Towdey. He was trying to buy the house.'

'Never heard of him.'

Agatha and Paul couldn't think of any more questions. They left after promising to let him know if they found out anything about the identity of the murderer.

'I still think of him as prime suspect,' said Agatha. 'I think we should contact that amateur theatrical group and find out if there was any way he could have got over to Hebberdon that evening.'

'It's that passage that's bothering me,' said Paul. 'The police must have gone over the whole house, even before her murder.'

'Before the murder, they probably didn't take her seriously enough to do any real search.'

'But after the murder?'

'Everything in that cellar was very dusty. Runcorn didn't impress me as the brain of Britain. Anyway, they'd open up the chest and just see curtains. You know what we should do, Agatha?'

'What?'

'We should go back there tonight with gloves on and go exactly everywhere we've been and wipe it clean. Then we can get Bill over and say we're sure an old house like that would have a secret passage and had they looked.'

'And while we're wiping it clean, we could be wiping away traces of the murderer as well.'

'Anyone with murder in mind would have got rid of fingerprints.'

'All right. But I hate the idea.'

At midnight that evening, Mrs Davenport stood screened by bushes at the end of Lilac Lane and peered along at the cottages of Paul and Agatha. She had been watching on and off all evening. Her patience was rewarded just as the church clock tolled out the last stroke of midnight. Paul Chatterton came out and went to Agatha's cottage. She came out. He kissed her on the cheek. He was carrying a travel bag. They both got into Agatha's car and drove off.

Juanita Chatterton has got to be told. It is my duty, Mrs Davenport told herself.

Chapter Seven

Agatha and Paul worked all night and into the next morning, dusting and wiping and vacuuming. When they left in daylight, they were too exhausted to care whether anyone saw them. The main thing was that they had removed all traces of their visit.

They agreed to go to bed and sleep and meet up in the evening to decide how they could tell the police about the passage.

Agatha's last dismal thought before she plunged down into sleep was that they were indeed a pair of amateurs, blundering around, without really knowing what they were doing.

They met in Agatha's kitchen at seven in the evening to plan what to do.

'An anonymous letter?' suggested Agatha.

'Maybe. There must be another way. I wonder whether Peter Frampton knew about the secret passage.'

'Perhaps. The person who did know was whoever put that chest over the trapdoor and put those curtains on top. It was a very old chest.'

'But it must have been moved at some time. The cellar can't have been full of junk from day one.'

'We could, you know,' said Agatha cautiously, 'throw ourselves on Bill's mercy.'

'Won't do. Breaking and entering. Destroying valuable evidence. There's no way he could cover up for us.'

'So what about an anonymous letter?'

'Risky. They can get your DNA off the envelope flap.'

'There are self-seal envelopes,' Agatha pointed out. 'I know, Moreton-in-Marsh police station is closed at certain times. Certainly, I think, during the night. We could just post a sheet of paper through the letter-box. Not typed. They used to be able to trace typewriters. Maybe they're able to trace computers. I've got a new packet of computer printing paper. It's a common brand.'

Paul sighed. 'Okay, let's try it. But we'd better wear gloves.'

Agatha went upstairs and extracted a pair of thin plastic gloves from a hair-dye kit she hadn't used and went back to join Paul.

They went through to her desk and Agatha put on the gloves and opened the packet of printing paper and gingerly extracted one sheet.

Holding it by the tips of two fingers, she carried it through to the kitchen. With her other hand, she tore off a sheet of kitchen paper and spread it on the kitchen table and then laid the sheet of paper down on it.

'What should I write?' she asked.

'Keep it simple,' said Paul. 'Block letters. Say: "There is a secret passage in Ivy Cottage. The entrance is at the bottom of an old chest in the cellar."'

Agatha tried to hold her breath as she wrote, terrified that even a drop of saliva would betray her to the forensics lab in Birmingham.

'There!' she said. 'Now how do we get it through the letter-box at the police station without being seen? There are flats for retired people bang opposite and some old person might be watching.'

'Fold it into a square,' said Paul. 'We'll need to think of some disguise.'

'Mrs Bloxby's got a box of costumes she keeps for the amateur dramatic company. Funny thing. They've just finished a production of *The Mikado*. She'll wonder why we want something. I don't even want to tell Mrs Bloxby about this.'

Paul said, 'I'll tell her we're going to a fancy dress party at a friend's in London.'

'If we wore the *Mikado* costumes, that would turn the police's attention back to Harry – that is, if they ever turned their attention off him.'

'Maybe there's something else. I don't think we should both dress up. All we need is one of us in disguise. Nothing dramatic.'

At two in the morning Agatha, wearing a bright red wig and a long droopy tea-dress – from a production of *The Importance of Being Earnest* – nervously walked round from the back road by the cricket ground where Paul had parked the car. A lorry rumbled past her on the Fosseway, but the driver was staring straight ahead. Moreton-in-Marsh seemed deserted. She scurried up to the police station and popped the note through the door.

She heaved a sigh of relief and started to hurry back. A hand caught her arm. 'Evenin', gorgeous.'

She swung round. A drunk man, small in stature, and far gone in drink, leered up at her. 'How's about a kiss?'

'Let go of me,' hissed Agatha.

The street lights shone on his glasses. They looked like two small orange moons in the light from the sodium lamps.

He was amazingly strong. He twisted her arm behind her back. 'Come 'ere,' he said thickly, his breath stinking of what smelt to the terrified Agatha like methylated spirits. She swung away from him and kneed him hard, right in his crotch. He let out an animal cry of pain and released her and then he started to scream. A light went on in the building opposite and Agatha picked up her skirts and ran.

Paul was standing by the car, looking anxiously down the road as Agatha ran towards him.

'Drive,' she panted. 'Get us out of here!'

They scrambled into the car and Paul shot off.

'What the hell . . .?' he began.

'A drunk,' said Agatha bitterly. 'I thought he was going to rape me. I hit him where it hurts most. That was what the screaming was about. Paul, we're blundering worse and worse. I think we should keep a low profile.'

'Suits me,' said Paul. 'I'm exhausted.'

Agatha felt miserable the following morning. She knew she was a successful public relations officer. She had thought she was a successful detective. Now, she felt like a failure. With the help of Paul, she had probably destroyed vital evidence. They had in their possession a valuable historical document. She suddenly groaned aloud. Why, oh, why had they not put the diary back where they had found it and left it for the police to find?

In the cottage next door, Paul's thoughts were pretty much the same – with one difference. He blamed Agatha. It was her fault she had got him embroiled in all this madness. He totally forgot that it had been his idea in the first place. What if they had left even half a fingerprint? He forgot that he had recently found Agatha attractive. Now he thought of her as a pushy middle-aged woman who might be mad. He had a longing to talk to his tempestuous wife, but when he phoned Madrid, her mother said she was out and she didn't know when Juanita would be back.

He had just replaced the receiver when the phone rang. 'Yes?' he said tentatively.

'Look, Paul, it's Agatha here. I was thinking . . .'

'I haven't time to talk to you at the moment,' he said harshly. 'Goodbye.'

Agatha slowly replaced the receiver and a fat tear rolled down one cheek. She felt old, stupid and very much alone. She decided to call on Mrs Bloxby. Not that she would tell her anything, but the vicar's wife was soothing company and her friendship unwavering.

Mrs Bloxby opened the door of the vicarage to her. 'Agatha?' she said. 'My dear, do come in and tell me what has upset you so much.'

Agatha burst into floods of tears. Mrs Bloxby piloted her into the living-room, pressed her down on the comfortable feather cushions of the old sofa, handed her a large box of Kleenex and then took her hand. Agatha dried her eyes and blew her nose. 'I feel such a fool,' she gulped. 'I shouldn't really be telling you anything.'

'You don't need to tell me anything if you don't want to,' said Mrs Bloxby in her kind voice. 'But do remember that I never repeat anything you say without your permission.'

In a halting voice, Agatha told her about the finding of the tunnel, the diary, and of how they had gone back and wiped everything so clean that any evidence had been destroyed. Then she told her about putting the anonymous note through the door of the police station and being attacked by the drunk man. 'I'll give you back the costume,' ended Agatha mournfully. 'I was disguised, you see. I was wearing a red wig and that tea-dress from *The Importance of Being Earnest*.'

Mrs Bloxby sat with her head bowed and her shoulders shaking. She let out a snort of laughter and then gave up and leaned back against the cushions and laughed and laughed.

'Mrs Bloxby!' Agatha half-rose to her feet, her face red with mortification.

'No, no.' Mrs Bloxby pulled Agatha back down. 'Don't you see how funny it is?'

Agatha gave a reluctant grin. 'Not funny, just stupid.'

Mrs Bloxby composed herself. 'I'll make some tea. We'll have tea and toasted teacakes in the garden because the sun has come out. Go into the garden and have a cigarette.'

Agatha, feeling calmer, went into the garden. A purple clematis tumbled down the mellow walls of the old vicarage behind her and in front of her the garden was a blaze of old-fashioned flowers: marigolds and stocks, delphiniums and lupins, gladioli and lilies.

She took out a packet of cigarettes and glared at it. How irritating to have one's life ruled by the compulsion to smoke. She put the packet away again.

Mrs Bloxby came out carrying a laden tray. 'Here we are. I made the teacakes myself.

I always think the shop ones don't have enough substance. Help yourself to milk and sugar.'

'There's something else,' said Agatha. 'There's Paul. I tried to phone him and he said he was busy and hung up on me.'

'He's probably feeling as frightened and silly as you are. But of course you must remember he's a man.'

'What's that got to do with it?'

'Men when they feel stupid and silly always look around for someone to blame.'

'That's very unfair!'

'Oh, he'll get over it. Let's look at the problem. The damage is done. But whoever frightened and murdered Mrs Witherspoon, assuming that one person did both, would be very careful to wear gloves. The police had no idea there was a secret passage and never would have done if you hadn't found it. So you have added to the investigation, rather than taken away from it.'

'I suppose,' mumbled Agatha, her mouth full of teacake.

'So tell me what else you have found out?'

Agatha described how Harry and Carol had asked them to investigate but had seemed reluctant to let them search the house and how Harry was going to share his inheritance with Carol.

'Why the change of heart?' asked Mrs Bloxby.

'Harry said that he and Carol had got together and found out how their mother had set one against the other. Seems believable.'

'Or it could be the action of a man guilty of

murder and desperate to put a good face on things.'

'If Paul hadn't gone off me, I was going to suggest going over to Mircester this evening to see if that amateur theatrical company are rehearsing anything and ask a few questions. There might have been an opportunity for Harry to disappear for a bit of the evening.'

'But in that case, wouldn't Harry himself be at the rehearsals?'

'You're right.'

'Wait a minute. I think I can find something out for you. I have a friend over in Mircester. I am sure she is part of the company.'

Mrs Bloxby went indoors. Agatha drank more tea and waited.

The vicar's wife came back and handed Agatha a slip of paper. 'Her name is Mrs Barley. That's her address. She's at home. If you go over now, you can have a chat with her.'

'Thanks a lot. Should I tell Paul?'

'No, leave him for a bit. He'll come round.'

Agatha went back to her cottage. Paul was working in his front garden. She hesitated as she passed, but although he was well aware of her, he didn't look up from his weeding. She shrugged and walked on.

Mrs Davenport avidly watched from the end of the lane. So it was over! She felt disappointed. She had still been trying to find out Juanita's address and had been looking forward to witnessing Agatha Raisin getting her come-uppance.

Agatha felt a burden had been lifted from her as she drove towards Mircester. She was on her own again and it felt good. Sex had impaired her usually brilliant detective abilities, she told herself.

She stopped in a lay-by outside Mircester and pulled a map of the town out of the glove compartment and worked out where Mrs Barley lived.

Barley was a nice name, reflected Agatha as she drove on into town. She would be a round, comfortable sort of countrywoman with apple cheeks and a generous bosom under a flowered apron.

The reality came as a shock. Mrs Barley – 'Do call me Robin' – was a thin woman in her sixties with expensively tinted golden hair wearing a Versace trouser suit and jangling with gold bangles.

'Come into my little sanctum,' she cooed. 'Do excuse the smell of paint.'

Agatha found herself in an artist's studio. A small white poodle with evil eyes ran barking at her ankles and Agatha resisted an urge to kick the beast away. There were canvases stacked against the walls and a half-finished painting on an easel. It showed a woman with a green-and-yellow face.

'A self-portrait,' murmured Robin Barley, spreading her long fingers in a deprecating gesture. 'A poor thing but mine own.'

'Looks great to me,' lied Agatha. Agatha was always puzzled by people who sneered at the

163

phrase: 'I don't know much about painting but I know what I like.' What on earth was up with that? Surely if one was buying a painting, one should choose what one liked. She had been told it was necessary to study art to appreciate it. Why? She wasn't an art student. James used to laugh at her and say she was comfortable in her philistinism, but she still couldn't see what it was all about. He had taken her to a Matisse exhibition and she had remarked loudly that she thought the painter's choice of colours ghastly and James had actually blushed and rushed her out of the gallery.

'The sun's over the yard-arm so we may as well have a drinkie,' said Robin. 'What's your poison?'

'Gin and tonic, please.'

'Absolutely. I'll have the same.' Robin went over to a small kitchen off the studio and fixed two drinks and carried them back. 'Bottoms up,' she said.

Agatha wondered whether Robin was capable of saying anything that wasn't hackneyed and clichéd.

'So you're the great detective,' said Robin. 'Sit down, please. I actually don't live here. This is my studio. I have a little pied-à-terre in Wormstone village. I am actually very busy at the moment but I never could refuse dear Margaret anything.'

'Margaret?'

'Mrs Bloxby, of course. So I thought, why not

grant you some of my precious time. It never rains but it pours,' she added obscurely.

'And every cloud has a silver lining,' said Agatha.

'And every road leads to the sea,' said Robin.

I wonder if she's mad, thought Agatha. Aloud she said, 'It's about Harry Witherspoon and *The Mikado*.'

Robin swept back her golden hair with one beringed hand. 'Ah, yes. I played Katisha.'

'The Daughter-in-Law Elect,' said Agatha, who knew her Gilbert and Sullivan.

'Exactly.'

'"There's a fascination frantic
In a ruin that's romantic;
Do you think you are sufficiently decayed?"'

quoted Agatha.

Robin gave a deprecating laugh. 'Actually, I brought glamour to the role. I always think it's a mistake to portray Katisha as ugly. But to your little problem. Harry was only a member of the chorus. I don't see how he could have found time to absent himself.'

'Would you notice?'

'There's a thing. Such an insignificant little man. No, I wouldn't. But the show ran from eight o'clock to nine-thirty. Then we all went to our dressing-rooms to take off make-up and get ready for the party. The party was on stage at the theatre. It went on until a little after midnight. Harry could easily have slipped out.'

'The police seem pretty sure he didn't, or rather that's the impression I got.'

'You poor thing. It must be awful for you, just dithering about the way you do without the resources of the police.'

'Yes, it can be infuriating trying to get information out of people like you.'

'Now, now,' chided Robin. 'Claws in. Little birds in their nests agree.'

Agatha picked up her handbag. 'Thanks for the drink. Better get going.'

'Please sit down. I could be of help to you.'

'How?' said Agatha, heading for the door.

'I can ask discreetly around. Harry was in the chorus and the chorus lot stick together. They all share the one dressing-room, the men, that is. One of them might have noticed if he'd gone AWOL.'

Agatha fished in her handbag and took out a card.

'Phone me if you discover anything,' she said.

'And if you do,' muttered Agatha as she got in her car, 'it'll be a bloody miracle.'

She treated herself to lunch in Mircester and then went round the shops before driving home.

Her heart sank as she turned into Lilac Lane and recognized Bill Wong's car. She parked and got out, only slightly relieved to see that Bill was on his own.

'We need to talk,' he said. 'And get your friend along here.'

Agatha did not want to say Paul wasn't speaking to her. 'Come inside,' she said. 'I'll phone him.'

She led the way into the kitchen. 'Switch on the percolator, Bill. I'll only be a moment.'

'Can't you use the extension in the kitchen?'

'Oh, yes,' said Agatha, flustered. 'Of course.' She picked up the receiver and then put it down again. 'I know why I was going to phone from the other room. My address book's in there. I've forgotten his phone number.'

'I've got it,' said Bill. He gave it to her and with a heavy heart Agatha picked up the phone. She hoped Paul would be out. What if he cracked and confessed to their breaking into Ivy Cottage? She was sure Bill now knew all about the anonymous note and suspected them.

But Paul answered on the first ring. 'It's Agatha,' she said brightly. 'Bill Wong is here and wants to talk to both of us.'

'What about?' demanded Paul sharply.

'Don't know. Hurry up.'

'But –'

Agatha replaced the receiver with a bang.

'I thought it was only people in movies who hung up without saying goodbye,' commented Bill.

'Didn't I say goodbye?' said Agatha and followed it with a stage laugh worthy of Robin Barley. 'So what's this all about?'

The doorbell rang. Agatha stood with her eyes fixed on Bill.

'That'll be Paul,' said Bill.

Agatha went to the door to let Paul in. To her dismay, Bill followed her. She had been hoping for a few hurried words of caution in private.

They all sat round the kitchen table, Agatha and Paul at one end and Bill facing them from the other. They had automatically taken up the same positions as they would have done during a police interrogation.

'There's something very puzzling has just emerged,' began Bill.

'Wouldn't anyone like coffee?' asked Agatha brightly.

'Later,' said Bill. Paul had his hands clasped and was studying the surface of the kitchen table.

'The thing is,' Bill went on, 'that the police received an anonymous note. It had been pushed through the door of Moreton police station. It said there was a secret passage leading from a chest in Ivy Cottage.'

'Goodness! So there is a secret passage!' exclaimed Agatha.

'Just like you suggested,' said Bill.

'Well, that must have been the way the murderer got in,' said Agatha. 'Ready for that coffee?'

'You don't seem curious as to why I am here,' remarked Bill.

'Obviously because it was our idea about the secret passage,' said Agatha, wishing Paul would raise his head and say something, anything – except the truth.

'I must ask you two if you had anything to do with this.'

'What are you talking about, Bill? Are you accusing us of having built a secret passage?'

'I think you know very well why I'm here. Harry Witherspoon has already been interviewed. He claims that as children they were never allowed down in the cellar. He says that you two had asked his permission to search the house, but that he had refused. You didn't break in, by any chance?'

'No,' said Agatha firmly. 'Was the house broken into?'

'Whoever did it had a key. No sign of a break-in.'

'Well, there you are,' said Agatha. 'It must have been Carol or Harry.'

'Furthermore,' pursued Bill, 'a woman in the flats next to Budgens supermarket heard screaming during the night. She looked out of her window and saw a woman struggling with a man. The woman kicked the man, who appeared to be drunk, and ran off. Our witness, when asked to describe the woman, said something most odd. She said that the woman struggling with the man was wearing what looked like an old-fashioned tea-gown. She says she has a photograph of her grandmother wearing one just like it. She could not tell us the colour of the woman's hair because those sodium lights change the colour of everything. Still, it sounds as if perhaps someone like you, Agatha, had got hold of some sort of theatrical costume as a disguise and gone to post that note.'

'Bill really! If we'd found a secret passage, we would have told you.'

'Not if you had found it by entering the house without permission.'

Paul raised his head and spoke for the first time. 'Is this an official inquiry?'

'No, it's a friendly call. If by any chance you did find that passage and destroyed any evidence, then you would be in deep trouble.'

Paul said quietly, 'Then it's just as well we didn't. No coffee for me, Agatha.' He suddenly smiled at her. 'Tea, please.'

Agatha felt herself go limp with relief. She rose to her feet and went to make tea and coffee.

'So tell us about the passage,' said Paul. 'Is it long? Is it very old? Where does it come out?'

'I'm not officially on this investigation,' said Bill. 'But I heard that it does lead from the bottom of a big old chest in the cellar, down some steps which had been repaired, and then along under the house and the garden and comes up through a trapdoor into the middle of shrubbery. The witness who saw the struggle near the police station phoned the police immediately. The local man turned out and found the note. A team of forensic experts have been working for hours. The passage and everything in the cellar had been dusted clean. A vacuum had been used. They have searched Carol's and Harry's homes and taken away their vacuums.'

Paul thought of the car vacuum he had used and which was now in a cupboard in his cottage. He hadn't even emptied it. Agatha thought of the tea-gown and wig upstairs.

Agatha placed a mug of coffee in front of Bill, glad to see her hand was steady. She then handed Paul a cup of tea.

'I suppose that dreadful Runcorn will be the next to call.'

'It's possible. As I say, I am not on the case. So whoever was frightening Mrs Witherspoon and then murdered her must have got into the house by way of the secret passage,' said Bill.

'If they're both one and the same person,' said Agatha.

Bill eyed her narrowly. He knew that in the past, just when Agatha seemed to be bumbling about in an infuriating way, she had been capable, nonetheless, of sudden flashes of intuition.

'I don't know,' said Agatha slowly. She took a mug of coffee for herself, lit a cigarette and sat down again. 'I think the murder was quite clever. If Mrs Witherspoon hadn't been so hale and hearty, it might well have been assumed it was an accident. When someone's very old, people don't inquire too closely into the reason for the death. If the doctor had signed the death certificate, the murderer would have been safe. Somehow, the haunting strikes me as a bit, well . . . childish. By the way, surely the police went over the house very carefully. Why didn't they look for a secret passage?'

171

'Because it didn't cross their minds. Runcorn is still sure Harry did it, so he hasn't even been looking in any other direction.'

Bill finished his coffee and got to his feet. 'Be careful, you two. I do hope you had nothing to do with this.'

'As if we would,' said Agatha and saw him out.

She hurried back to the kitchen. 'That tea-gown and wig. I'd better get them back to Mrs Bloxby.'

'And the vacuum. I'll throw it away. We'd better wash all the clothes we had on last night. Look, Agatha, I'm sorry I was so rude to you, but I couldn't believe we had been so stupid.'

'You can take me for dinner later. Let's get rid of the evidence . . . now.'

By early evening, Agatha was just comforting herself with the thought that the wig and tea-gown were back in the vicarage and that the clothes she had worn while they were cleaning the cellar and passage were all clean and dry and the shoes she had worn had been thoroughly washed and cleaned when the phone rang. It was Paul. 'Runcorn's here,' he said in a low voice. 'He wants you to step along.'

Agatha, with feet like lead, made her way along to Paul's cottage. Detective Inspector Runcorn and Sergeant Evans were waiting for her in Paul's living-room. Paul was sitting quietly at his desk.

'Right, Mrs Raisin. Sit down,' ordered Runcorn.

Agatha seized a hard chair and placed it next to Paul and sat down.

'Where were both of you last night between the hours of two a.m. and three a.m.?'

'In bed,' said Agatha and Paul at the same time.

'Any witnesses?'

'No,' said Agatha coldly.

'I am particularly interested in your movements, Mrs Raisin.' Runcorn fixed her with a hard stare. 'Someone put a note through the door of the Moreton police station. The note stated that there was a secret passage in Ivy Cottage.'

'And is there?' asked Paul. Again Agatha felt relief.

'Yes, there is, and everything has been wiped clean. A vacuum was used as well. We can get a search warrant but I would like the vacuums from both your houses.'

'Okay,' said Agatha quickly, not wanting them to come back with a warrant and search her whole cottage in case they found something incriminating, like a strand of wig hair.

'Mr Chatterton?'

Paul shrugged. 'All right with me.'

He rose and went to a cupboard under the stairs and pulled out an upright vacuum cleaner. Sergeant Evans wrote out a receipt.

'I'll go and get mine,' said Agatha.

'If you have a vacuum for the car, bring that as well,' ordered Runcorn.

'I don't have one of those,' said Agatha over her shoulder.

She was back in a very short time, still uneasy about leaving Paul alone with them. She sensed Runcorn was disappointed by their apparent eagerness to help.

But curiosity prompted her to ask, 'What makes you think we could have anything to do with it? Why on earth would we want to murder Mrs Witherspoon?'

'There's a legend that a fortune was hidden in that old house. With Mrs Witherspoon dead and the house empty, some crazy people might have decided to go on a treasure hunt.'

'Whereas the intelligent interpretation would be that the killer went back to make sure he had left no traces,' said Paul.

'And left a note at the police station?'

'Could be someone else. Could be someone who knows the murderer.'

'Ah, that reminds me. A witness said that the woman who left the note, or rather, some woman who was having a fight with a drunk, was wearing an old-fashioned tea-gown. Do you possess such an item, Mrs Raisin?'

'I'm not old enough.'

'But you would not mind if Sergeant Evans here took a look in your wardrobe?'

'He can look now if he likes.'

When Agatha had left, Runcorn leaned forward and said in a man-to-man voice, 'Now, Mr Chatterton, sir, that is a woman who has interfered in police investigations before. It would go badly for you if you were found to be involved. Wouldn't mind an excuse to put her away for a bit and keep her out of mischief. So you can tell me. What's she been up to?'

'Mrs Raisin is a neighbour and a friend of mine,' said Paul. 'It was entirely my idea to investigate the haunting of Mrs Witherspoon. Mr Harry Witherspoon and his sister, Carol, asked us after the funeral to help to find the murderer.'

Runcorn's face darkened. 'I hope you didn't agree.'

'We said we would do what we could. Nothing we do can possibly interfere with your investigations. If we do find out anything of significance, we will fell you immediately.' Paul glanced nervously towards the bookshelves where the diary was in plain view, placed among glossy new books on computer science.

'Take my advice and don't do anything at all.'

They sat in silence until Agatha returned with Evans. 'Nothing,' said the sergeant.

Runcorn rose to his feet. 'That will be all . . . for now.'

'Phew!' said Agatha when they had left. 'That was hairy.'

'Something's puzzling me,' said Paul.

'What?'

'It was so dusty in the cellar, as if nothing

175

had been moved for years. I think Runcorn's in trouble. I think the police just looked around the cellar and didn't do a proper search.'

'Probably. But you would think the murderer would have left some trace.'

'You know,' said Paul, 'I think we should try to have a word with Harry and Carol tomorrow. I cannot believe that two people brought up in that house, however bullied, didn't explore the cellar.'

'But would two children find that false bottom in the trapdoor?'

'Maybe not. And I've just remembered something. That trapdoor leading up to the garden, it was fairly new. It looks as if someone had stumbled across the way in and decided it was a useful way of having secret access to the house.'

'We're forgetting about Peter Frampton,' said Agatha. 'He's a local historian. He might have found out about it and he might have known where to look. Remember, he wanted to buy the house. I think we should try to find out a bit more about him.'

'Right. But we'll have that dinner first and then tackle Harry and Carol.'

Robin Barley sat in front of the mirror in her dressing-room that evening after a dress rehearsal of *Macbeth*, in which she had played Lady Macbeth, feeling her ego had been thoroughly bruised. It had been an exciting day playing detective, making multiple phone calls to ascertain whether Harry could have slipped out. And he could have! Should she tell that Raisin trout creature? No, she would persevere and then go to the police, first making sure that the *Mircester Chronicle* got a full story of her own detective abilities. Then she remembered the horror of the dress rehearsal and her face darkened. That new producer was a drunken beast. Why on earth had their usual producer, Guy Wilson, taken it upon himself to go off with shingles? And why did they have to end up with a failed Stratford producer who had decided to set the whole of *Macbeth* in Bosnia, with the clansmen wearing gas masks? He had told her in front of the whole cast that she had made Lady Macbeth sound like some lady of the manor opening a church fête.

The door of her dressing-room opened and a face covered with a gas mask peered round it. Robin turned round and scowled. She did not associate much with the foot soldiers of the cast.

But he eased in, carrying a splendid bunch of red roses. 'To match your beauty,' he said, his voice muffled behind the mask.

Robin suddenly beamed. 'You are a love. What beautiful flowers!'

'I see you've a vase over there. I'll just pop them in for you.'

'You haven't told me your name,' said Robin.

Chapter Eight

Agatha whistled happily the following morning as she prepared a breakfast of toast and marmalade and black coffee. The sun streamed in through the open kitchen door and all was right with her world. She and Paul had enjoyed a pleasant dinner. Once more they were at ease in each other's company. They had even begun to joke about their amateur mistakes. She had told him about her visit to Robin Barley and had even done an imitation of her that had made Paul laugh.

He was to call for her that afternoon and then they were going to go to Towdey to see if they could find out more about Peter Frampton.

Once more her head was beginning to fill with rosy dreams. She had not yet had time to visit the hairdresser's, so after breakfast she went up to the bathroom and used a brunette rinse on her hair to soften the effect of red roots.

Wrapping a towel round her hair, she went downstairs again and sat in the garden to enjoy the sun.

A frantic ringing on the doorbell, followed by a hammering on the front door, made her spring to her feet.

She ran through the house and opened the door. Paul stood there. 'Agatha, Agatha, did you say you had been to see someone called Robin Barley?'

'Yes, come in. What's up?'

'I just heard it on the radio. I was driving back from Moreton when I heard she'd been found dead in her dressing-room.'

They walked through to the kitchen as Agatha said, 'Maybe she had a heart attack.'

'The news report said the police are treating the death as suspicious.'

Agatha sank down on a kitchen chair and looked at him bleakly.

'Sooner or later the police are going to question the neighbours around her studio and they'll give a description of me. But if she was killed in her dressing-room, that points again to Harry. Oh, dear. It's all my fault. She was so keen to play detective.'

'Did you encourage her to play detective?'

'Not really. In fact, she was so bitchy I was just glad to get out of there.'

'So it's not your fault. No point in trying to see Harry or Carol today, and it would be better to leave Peter Frampton until we find out more. It must have something to do with Harry.'

'If it isn't Harry,' said Agatha, 'and if he has an

alibi, then her murder may not have anything to do with the Witherspoon one.'

'Perhaps we should try to see Bill Wong.'

'I should think every detective they've got will be out on this one and they'll be under pressure from the media. This one's more exotic than an old lady being murdered.'

'I feel there's something we should be doing.'

The doorbell rang again. They looked at each other in dismay. 'Must be the police,' said Agatha dismally.

But when she answered the door it was to find a distressed Mrs Bloxby. 'Come in,' said Agatha. 'We've just heard.'

'I cannot believe it,' said Mrs Bloxby. 'I've known Mrs Barley quite a long time. Did you see her?'

'Yes, I told her we were trying to find out if Harry could have had a chance to slip away and get over to Hebberdon. I know she was a friend of yours, but she was . . . difficult.'

'Poor Robin could be rather grandiose,' said the vicar's wife, 'but she had a heart of gold underneath it all. She did a lot of good work for the church. I phoned the rector of Saint Ethelburgh's in Wormstone, the village where she lived. He had an arrangement to meet her in her dressing-room after the dress rehearsal. She was going to produce a play for the village church. It was he who found her.

'He said she was lying near the door. Her face was an awful colour and she had vomited. He called the ambulance and the police and the fire brigade, all three he was in such a state. The police arrived first. He was told to wait outside. Then he was driven to police headquarters and told to wait there. When two detectives finally arrived to interview him, he said it was a terrible ordeal. They kept asking him over and over again if he had brought her flowers. And he had to repeat over and over again that he had not brought her any flowers. He had an arrangement to meet her and when he knocked on the dressing-room door and did not get a reply, he had opened the door and found her. It came out at the end of the interview that poor Mrs Barley had died of cyanide poisoning and the police think that hydrogen cyanide pellets were dropped into a vase of roses. The resultant cyanide gas released by the pellets killed her.'

'How on earth in this day and age in the quiet Cotswolds would someone get hold of cyanide?' asked Agatha.

'Farmers used to use hydrogen cyanide,' said Paul. 'But it's now banned, along with DDT. I suppose there must be some of the stuff still lying around.'

'So what do we do now?' asked Agatha.

'I think we wait,' said Paul.

'I wish we had the resources of the police,' mourned Agatha. 'We can't check phone bills and see who she'd been phoning.'

'There are detective agencies who can get you a three-month record of anyone's phone bill,' said Mrs Bloxby, surprising them. 'It costs about four hundred pounds plus VAT.'

'Wow, how do you know this?' asked Agatha.

Mrs Bloxby coloured slightly. 'I'm afraid it's confidential. A parishioner was very obsessed with some woman and he wanted to check on her phone calls to see if she had been phoning an old lover, although she swore she hadn't.'

'And had she?' asked Agatha, fascinated.

'Oh, yes.'

'And that cured his obsession?'

'No, it got worse. He finally moved to Australia. Such a waste of money.'

Agatha racked her brains to think of any parishioner who had moved to Australia. Mrs Bloxby smiled slightly. 'Before your time, Mrs Raisin.'

'You know,' said Agatha, 'I think I should phone Bill and tell him about my visit to Robin. I've a feeling they're going to find out anyway.'

'You'll get an awful grilling from Runcorn,' Paul pointed out.

'I'll get less of a grilling if I volunteer the information,' said Agatha.

She went into the other room to phone.

Agatha came back after a few minutes. 'I got Bill. He's on the case at last. I've to go in right away to headquarters.'

Paul drove Agatha to police headquarters. They were told to wait and then Agatha was taken

183

away to an interviewing room. She sat for almost a quarter of an hour looking down at the scarred table, at the institution-green walls, and at the small frosted glass window until the door opened and Bill walked in, followed by Evans.

He went through the ritual of switching on the tape before sitting down with Evans and facing Agatha.

'Now, Mrs Raisin,' he said formally, 'you phoned me to say that you had seen the deceased, Mrs Robin Barley, yesterday.'

'That is correct.'

'At what time?'

'I think it was just before lunchtime. I can't be sure. Say about twelve o'clock.'

'Had you known Mrs Barley before?'

'No.'

'How did you happen to be visiting her?'

'I wondered if it might have been possible for Harry Witherspoon to leave the performance and go to Hebberdon on the night of his mother's murder. Mrs Bloxby –'

'That is the wife of the vicar of Saint Peter and Saint Paul in Carsely?'

'You know that, Bill.'

'For the tape,' snapped Evans.

'Yes. Anyway, I wanted to get in touch with a member of the cast of *The Mikado*. Mrs Bloxby said she had a friend, Mrs Robin Barley, who might be able to help me. She phoned her and gave me her address. So I went to her studio.'

'And did she have any information?'

'No, I found her a rather silly woman. She said she would phone around other members of the cast to find out if Harry could have slipped away. I was fed up with her because she had been rude to me. I was only there a very short time. I gave her my card and told her to phone me if she found out anything, and then I left.'

'And after that?' asked Evans.

'I treated myself to lunch at Pam's Kitchen in the main street. Then I walked around the shops. I got back home and was interviewed by you detectives. After you had left, Paul – Mr Chatterton – and I went out for dinner.'

'Where?'

'The Churchill over at Paxford.'

'And how long did that take?'

'Let me think. We booked the table for eight o'clock. We didn't leave until ten-thirty. We went to my cottage and had a nightcap and then Mr Chatterton went to his cottage at around midnight.'

Evans spoke. 'You have got to stop interfering, Mrs Raisin. You will not leave the country. You will be prepared for further questioning.'

'Okay.'

Bill stood up. 'That will be all for the moment.'

'Bill . . .?' Agatha started.

He shook his head briefly and Evans escorted Agatha out.

'So how did it go?' asked Paul as they walked away from police headquarters.

'Not as awful as I expected, because Bill himself interviewed me. But, oh Paul, he looked so hard-faced and disapproving.'

'Having a friend like you must be a serious embarrassment for a police detective at times.'

'I hope he hasn't gone off me,' fretted Agatha. 'He was my first friend – since I moved down here,' she added hurriedly, not wanting Paul to know that the prickly Agatha Raisin hadn't had any friends before that.

'He'd come around if we could do anything to solve this case,' said Paul.

'Fat chance of that.' Agatha's mobile phone began to ring. She pulled it out of her handbag.

She listened intently and then said excitedly, 'Keep him there. We'll be as fast as we can.'

Agatha rang off and said to Paul, 'That was Mrs Bloxby. She's got that rector with her, the one that found the body.'

Together, they sprinted to the car.

Mrs Bloxby ushered them through the vicarage and into the garden, where a thin white-haired man was drinking tea.

'Mrs Raisin, may I introduce Mr Potter, rector of Saint Ethelburgh's? Mr Potter, Mrs Raisin and Mr Chatterton.'

They all sat down. Agatha studied the rector. He had a thin, gentle face and mild eyes. His shoulders were stooped and his fingers deformed with arthritis.

'I agreed to see you,' he said in a beautiful voice, the old Oxford English rarely heard these days. 'I would normally shrink from the idea of any amateur detection, but that man Runcorn annoyed me. He is brutal and stupid. Mrs Bloxby speaks highly of your powers of detection.'

'Tell us what happened,' urged Agatha.

'I should not speak ill of the dead, but I did find Mrs Barley a rather exhausting and over-powering woman. But, as Mrs Bloxby will agree, she was a first-class fund-raiser for the church. She was going to put on a play in the church hall in Wormstone.' He gave a little smile. 'She was, of course, going to play the lead.'

'What was the play going to be?' asked Agatha with a sudden feeling of foreboding.

'*The Importance of Being Earnest.*'

'In Edwardian costume?'

'Yes, indeed.' Agatha shot a miserable glance at Paul. So they had muddied the waters of the investigation even further. The police would assume that Robin had been the woman in the tea-gown.

'In any case,' the vicar went on, 'I had agreed to see her in her dressing-room. There was absolutely no reason why we could not have met the following morning, but Mrs Barley liked receiving visitors in her dressing-room. As I told Mrs Bloxby, I knocked at the dressing-room door, and getting no reply, I walked in.' He went on to describe what he had told Mrs Bloxby earlier.

'The police say it was cyanide poisoning.

187

Someone took her a bouquet of flowers, put them in a vase of water and slipped the pellets of hydrogen cyanide into the water.'

'I wonder whether her death has anything to do with Mrs Witherspoon's murder,' said Agatha.

'Why not?' asked Paul.

'Just suppose it isn't Harry who's guilty,' said Agatha. 'Then what possible reason could anyone have for murdering Robin? Did she have any enemies, Mr Potter?'

'Not that I know of. But amateur theatrical companies can be amateur in everything but temperament. There are as many feuds and jealousies as there are in the real theatre. You see, poor Mrs Barley could not act.'

'Good heavens,' said Agatha. 'Then why did she have a major part in *Macbeth*?'

'She was a very rich woman. Most of the funding for the Mircester Players came from her. In return, she demanded lead roles. I remember once there was a dreadful scene when they were rehearsing a Christmas production of *Oklahoma*. As usual, Mrs Barley insisted on playing the lead.'

'You mean the young girl in the surrey with the fringe on top?'

'The same. The female members of the cast confronted her. Mrs Barley had a dreadful singing voice. They told her she was too old for the part and could not sing. She would not back down until one of them played a recording of her singing. Even Mrs Barley had to admit it was awful.'

'Who led the protest?' asked Agatha.

'A Miss Emery. Miss Maisie Emery. She got the part and was very good in it, too.'

'But Robin told me she was playing Katisha in *The Mikado*!'

'Mrs Barley got away with that because Katisha is meant to be ugly and her voice threatening.'

'Dear me. Do you know where we could find Miss Emery?'

'I don't think she could have had anything to do with it,' said Mr Potter.

'But she might know someone or something,' Paul pointed out.

'I do not know her address, but I know she works at the Midlands and Cotswolds Bank in Mircester.'

'Back to Mircester,' groaned Paul, as they set out again. 'We're clutching at straws.'

'It's better than sitting around doing nothing,' said Agatha. She looked out of the car window as they cruised down Fish Hill. Black clouds were covering the Malvern Hills. 'Rats! I think it's going to rain.'

'Never mind,' said Paul, who was driving. 'I've got a couple of umbrellas in the back.'

'Quite the Boy Scout, aren't you? Prepared for

everything. It's getting late. Think she'll still be at the bank?'

'They close at four-thirty, but they stay at work until around five-thirty to do the books or whatever bank people do.'

They arrived outside the bank just before five-thirty. 'There are lights on inside,' said Agatha. 'Wait and see who comes out.'

They waited by the door. Exactly at five-thirty, several women came out. 'Miss Emery?' Agatha asked them.

'Maisie'll be out in a moment,' said one.

A thin girl with a rabbity face appeared a few minutes later. 'Miss Emery?' asked Agatha.

'Yes, what do you want? The bank's closed.'

'It's nothing to do with banking,' said Agatha. 'It's about the murder of Mrs Robin Barley.'

Her mouth dropped farther open, exposing long irregular teeth. 'Robin! *Murdered!*'

'Yes, last night. In her dressing-room. Didn't you know? Weren't you at the theatre?'

'No, there wasn't a part for me. They wanted to put me in a gas mask to play one of the soldiers, but I knew Robin had suggested that to humiliate me, so I told them to stuff it.'

'But surely one of the customers said something. It must be all over the town.'

'No. One of them, mind, said he'd heard there had been an accident at the theatre, that's all.'

Paul said, 'Would you like to come for a drink with us? We'd like to ask you about Robin.'

She looked at them suspiciously. In that

moment, Agatha felt the loss of her one-time friend, Sir Charles Fraith. She had only to mention his title and people always talked to them.

'Let me introduce ourselves,' said Agatha. 'I am Mrs Agatha Raisin and this is Mr Paul Chatterton. We are helping the police with their inquiries.' And that was true enough, thought Agatha.

Paul smiled charmingly at Maisie and she visibly thawed. 'All right, then,' she said. 'But I don't like going into common pubs. There's a cocktail bar in the George Hotel.'

The cocktail bar in the George was more like a fusty little overfurnished ante-room with a small bar manned by an ancient barman. Maisie said she would like a vodka and Red Bull and showed a tendency to sulk when the barman informed them with a gleam of surly pleasure that he did not stock Red Bull. Paul quickly suggested she try something more exotic and ordered a cocktail for her called a Sunrise Special. Maisie looked pleased with the choice when she was served a tall blue drink with dusty little paper umbrellas sticking out of the top. Agatha privately thought those umbrellas had done the rounds more than once.

'So what can you tell us about Robin?' asked Paul.

'How did she die?'

'Cyanide poisoning. Someone gave her a

bouquet of flowers and slipped cyanide pellets into a vase of water. The gas that came off killed her.'

Maisie's eyes gleamed with excitement. 'Well, I never! Where was this? At that studio of hers?'

'No, in her dressing-room after the dress rehearsal. Did she have any enemies?'

Agatha was happy for once to let Paul take over the questioning. Maisie was already casting flirtatious little looks at him.

'She had loads of people who hated her. The audience was mostly made up of friends and relatives. She was turning us into a joke. Some of the gay boys in this town would turn up, mind you, just for a laugh. I tried to tell the producer that we wouldn't need her money if we could put on decent shows, but she paid an awful lot for costumes and scenery and she owned the theatre.'

'Where did she get her money from?' asked Paul.

'The late Mr Barley owned a chain of super-markets. When he died, she sold them all for millions.'

'Did anyone dislike her more than the others?'

'Reckon we were all pretty much the same. But I mean, none of us would have *poisoned* her. We wouldn't know how.'

'Was Harry Witherspoon at the dress rehearsal?' asked Agatha.

'I dunno. I don't see why he should have been.

He'd just have been one of the clansmen or soldiers, you see.'

'Wasn't he usually in a small part anyway?' asked Agatha.

'Well, it was his asthma and hay fever, you see. First, he didn't want to wear a gas mask. He said he couldn't breathe properly. Then this idiot of a producer, well, when Birnam wood's supposed to come to Dunsinane, instead of carrying tree branches, the soldiers were to carry bouquets of flowers. Someone asked him why. He said it was to highlight the atrocities of war. Prick!' she added with venom. 'Any chance of another of these?' She held up her empty glass.

'I'll get it,' said Agatha.

The barman was sitting reading a newspaper and showed no signs of paying any attention to Agatha Raisin until she thumped her fist on the bar and shouted, 'Service!'

'And this producer, what's his name?'

'Brian Welch.'

'And what's his history?' Paul asked as Agatha returned, triumphant, having made the barman decorate Maisie's cocktail with fresh paper umbrellas.

'Who are we talking about?' asked Agatha.

'The producer, Brian Welch. I was just asking what his background was.'

'He said he used to produce for the Royal Shakespeare Company,' said Maisie, 'but someone said he was only the producer for some amateur production in Stratford. He loathed Robin.'

'You don't know where he's living, do you?' asked Paul.

'No, but when he's not in the theatre, he spends his time in the Crown.'

'And what does he look like?'

'Small and fat. Wears tacky clothes. Got a lot of fair hair.'

They asked her more questions but without gaining much of importance, and then said goodnight to her and set out for the Crown, which Agatha remembered was one of Mircester's seedier hostelries.

The first person they saw in the nearly deserted pub was a man answering Maisie's description.

They went up to him and Paul asked, 'Mr Welch?'

'Yes. Who wants to know?'

Paul performed the introductions and explained what they were doing.

'Can't you leave that sort of thing to the police?' he demanded, glaring at his empty glass.

'What are you drinking?' asked Agatha quickly.

'Whisky.'

'A double?'

He suddenly smiled. 'Sure.' Agatha went to the bar thinking that at one time that pudgy face would not have been swollen and covered in

194

broken veins and he might have been an attractive man.

She returned with his drink, and soft drinks for herself and Paul, in time to hear Paul saying, 'But it couldn't have been suicide.'

'I wouldn't put it past her. Cheers! That bitch seemed out to wreck the show.' He viciously mimicked Robin's voice. '"You have no conception of history." Pah! Silly cow. I gave her a dressing-down in front of the cast to try to get some humility into her. She couldn't act.'

'Wasn't that dangerous?' asked Agatha. 'She had the power to sack you, didn't she? I mean, she was the money behind the whole thing. She hired you, didn't she?'

'Yes, but I got a contract out of her, so she could do bugger all about it.'

'Why Bosnia?' asked Agatha.

'That's what she kept asking. Don't you see, that whole play is about the abuse of military might?'

Agatha decided to leave that one. 'I gather Harry Witherspoon wasn't in the cast.'

'Oh, that little shopkeeper who murdered his mother? No. He was beefing about his hay fever and asthma.'

Agatha sat up straight. 'Blast! Why didn't I think of it before?'

'What?' asked Paul.

'Gas masks, of course. Not only a disguise, but a protection against gas. Robin would just think it was one of the cast. But it needn't have been. Could have been anyone from outside.'

'You'll need to ask Freddy, who mans the stage door.'

'Where can we find him?'

'If the police aren't grilling him, you'll find him at his digs in Coventry Road. Little cottage at the end.'

'Where's Coventry Road?' asked Paul.

'It's nearly in the country on our road out. One of the roads leading off the Fosse. I'll tell you when to turn off.'

'We never ask the right questions,' mourned Paul.

'Like what?'

'Simple ones. Like what's Freddy's second name? What kind of person is he?'

'We'll soon find out,' said Agatha. 'Turn off down here on the left, just past that garage.'

Paul swung round into Coventry Road and they cruised along slowly, past shops and council houses. 'We're nearly out into the country,' said Paul. 'I don't see any cottage.'

'Try round the next bend.'

'There it is,' said Paul.

A little white cottage stood on its own by the road. 'And that's another thing we should have asked,' said Paul. 'What's his phone number? He may be out for the evening.'

'Stop complaining. We'll soon find out.'

A worried-looking woman with her hair in curlers answered the door. 'We're looking for Freddy, the stage-door keeper,' said Agatha.

'Dad's at his allotment. Who's asking?'

Patiently Agatha went through the whole thing again. 'He's a bit shaken up about things. You'd best leave him alone.' And with that she slammed the door in their faces.

'Well, at least we know he's at some allotments. Let's ask along the road. Someone at that garage might know where the allotments are.'

At the garage, a man volunteered the information that the allotments were off Barney Lane. 'Can't miss them,' he said. 'Go back to Haydon's Close on your right, go along a few yards, make a left down Blackberry Road, then second right is Barney Lane.'

They made a few false turns, Agatha having forgotten the instructions and Paul unfairly saying that women never knew how to navigate to cover up the fact he had forgotten most of the instructions himself. At last they found the allotments, little strips of land where men were tending vegetables.

They asked the first man they came across for Freddy, and he jerked his thumb towards an old man who was bent over a vegetable bed.

They approached him and went through the usual preamble of who they were and why they wanted to speak to him. 'Freddy Edmonds,' he said, holding out an earthy hand which they both shook.

197

'Come into my office,' he said, a grin creasing up the wrinkles on his face.

His 'office' was a shed beside his strip of allotment where lines of lettuce, cabbage, spinach, potatoes and various other plants they did not recognize were stretched out in neat rows.

He sat on a box, removed a greasy cap from his head, and pulled a pipe out of his pocket. Paul sat on another box and Agatha on an old car seat.

'The police have been at me earlier,' he began, stuffing tobacco from a tin into his pipe. Agatha often wondered why anyone could be bothered smoking a pipe. There was always all that work of getting it filled, tamping the tobacco down, lighting it, then lighting it again frequently when it went out, and then scraping out the resultant mess from the bowl only to start the process again.

'They were asking me if anyone went in through the stage door while the performance was on. I told them, no one. First one was that reverend who came to see Mrs Barley.'

'And what about people leaving? I mean, you would notice if someone walked past you still in costume? You see, it could have been someone not in the cast, but wearing a gas mask.'

'Well, you see,' he said, exhaling a cloud of foul-smelling smoke, 'when the reverend raised the alarm, they were all still in their dressing-rooms, and the police, they arrived in minutes and two were left to guard the stage door.'

'And is there no other way out?'

'Not a one. They go past me or not at all.'

There was a long silence and then Agatha said, 'It must be a very boring job. Have you always done it?'

'No, I worked on the railway until I retired. Saw an ad in the local paper and got the job. I remember when it was the Gaiety Theatre in the old days. It was lying empty for quite a bit until Mrs Barley bought it.'

'Yes, we've just learned she actually bought it.'

'I was hoping they'd call it the Gaiety like the old vaudeville days, but it's just the Mircester Players, and amateurs at that. Still, it's a job.'

Above Freddy's head was a shelf crammed with gardening books and magazines.

'You read a lot about gardening,' said Paul.

'Everything I can get.'

Agatha had a sudden mental picture of Freddy, sitting in his cubicle at the stage door – bound to be a sort of cubicle, they all were – and avidly reading some book or magazine on gardening while a shadowy figure slipped silently past him.

'It was a warm evening,' she said. 'Was the street door open?'

'Yes, I had to let some air in.'

'So you wouldn't hear anyone come in?'

'I'd hear their footsteps and look up.'

'Could someone have got past you at a crouch – under your line of vision?'

'I s'pose they could,' he said uneasily.

'Didn't you have to go for a pee?' asked Paul.

He puffed at his pipe for a long moment. 'That I did. But I shut and locked the outside door while I went off.'

'And how often did you go?' asked Agatha.

'Three times. My bladder ain't what it used to be. Age. You know what it's like.'

'Not yet,' said Agatha frostily.

'And you shut the door each time you went?' asked Paul.

Another long silence while Freddy puffed energetically on his pipe. 'Sure I did,' he said.

'Tell us about Robin Barley,' said Agatha. 'Did anyone really hate her?'

'She got up the noses of a lot of people, that's for sure. But they're all a bunch of prima donnas. Sometimes I come across them in their day jobs, at the bank or in the shops, and they're as quiet as mice. But the minute they get in their theatre, they all think they're Alec Guinness and Edith Evans.'

'Did you know Robin very well?'

'As well as anyone, I suppose,' said Freddy. 'Mind you, she did a lot of good work for the church, and let's face it, without her money there wouldn't be any Mircester Players and I wouldn't have a job. She loved the theatre. When she interviewed me, I felt she saw me as a character part – good old Freddy, touching his forelock at the stage door as the star went by. So I acted the way she wanted me.'

'What did you do when you were working on

the railways?' asked Agatha, suddenly feeling that Freddy in his way was as much an actor as the rest of them.

'I was an area manager.'

'I think you are a very clever man,' observed Agatha. 'Why the allotment?'

'I love growing things. It's peaceful here. No one to bother me.'

'I suppose the show is suspended?'

'It'll open tomorrow. That producer, he thinks Robin's murder should bring a good audience and he's anxious to cash in on it. Maisie Emery's playing Lady Macbeth.'

'Robin was a widow. Did she have any male friends? Was she going out with anyone?'

'Not that I heard. I did hear she was a great joiner of things, getting one enthusiasm after another and letting it drop – Pilates, transcendental meditation, salsa, you name it.'

Agatha produced her card and gave it to him. 'If you do hear anything, let us know.'

'I don't feel that was a waste of time,' said Agatha as they drove home. 'He's very sharp. When he first said he'd been working on the railway, what with his pipe and his greasy cap and his old gardemng clothes, I thought he might have had something to do with repairing the tracks. But when I listened to him, I realized he was much brighter than I'd first thought.'

'Don't be snobbish, Agatha. I am sure there are bright labourers all over the place.'

'No, it's you who's being snobbish.'

The argument occupied them all the way home.

Outside Agatha's cottage, Paul said, 'Enough about the working-man. Where do we go from here? I'm stumped.'

'We'll sleep on it,' said Agatha. Unusually for her, she wanted to be alone. There was something diminishing about spending so much time with a man who did not flirt. 'I'll see you tomorrow.'

She let herself into her cottage, petted her cats and turned them out into the garden. She was relieved for once to get a break from blundering around, asking people questions, trying to get a breakthrough.

Agatha ferreted in the freezer and took out a frost-encrusted package and deposited it in the microwave. She took it out when the bell pinged and noticed it was a Marks & Spencer's lasagne. Could be worse, she thought, and turned the microwave on to full heat. After she had eaten, she cooked a couple of herring for her cats, not seeing the irony in a woman who would cook fresh food for her cats but not for herself.

Chapter Nine

Agatha did not hear from Paul the next morning, and found herself reluctant to call on him or phone him. She was suffering from delayed shock over the death of Robin Barley and felt angry, guilty and obscurely responsible. Who would be the next to go because of her interference? The stage-door man, Freddy?

On impulse, she locked up her cottage and drove to London. She went to a beautician in Bond Street that she had patronized in the old days when she was living in London. They told her they were fully booked but she became so cross and irritable that when the receptionist happened – 'By a miracle, sweeties,' as she told her flatmates that evening, 'I thought she was going to *assault* me!' – to receive a phone call cancelling an appointment in the middle of Agatha's tirade, she gladly booked her in.

Agatha submitted herself to a full treatment of non-surgical face-lift, body wrap and leg wax before emerging some hours later feeling rejuvenated. She wandered around Fenwick's and fell in love with a pink chiffon dress and bought it, despite the warning voices in her head telling her that at her age she would look like the late Barbara Cartland. For once, she enjoyed being back in London, enjoyed the buzz of being in a big city. She secured a table at one of London's most fashionable restaurants by dint of booking the table under the name of the Duchess of Cromarty. She finished a lavish meal with a portion of the restaurant's famous chocolate cream pie and then made her way back to where she had parked her car, feeling that the meal had negated all the good of the body wrap. Her skirt felt tight at the waistband.

On the road home, a horrendous accident resulting in a tailback along the M40 caused her an hour's delay. All the well-being she had experienced at escaping from Carsely left her. She fretted about her cats. She should never have left them locked up inside all day.

As she turned down the Carsely road, she warred with herself. One part of her mind was telling her to leave well alone. The other part was telling her that if she could find out anything about the murders, then it might cancel out some of the guilt she felt over the blunder of finding the secret passage and cleaning it up and over Robin's death. As she got out of the car, she noticed that the thick curtains which covered her living-room windows were tightly closed. She must have forgotten to pull them back before she left.

She let herself into her cottage and paused in the darkness of the hall. No cats came to greet her. She put out her hand towards the light switch and then stared in horror at the closed door of her sitting-room. A light was shining from under the door. Terror made her behave stupidly. Instead of retreating to her car, driving off and calling the police, or running next door to get help from Paul, she seized a stout walking-stick from a stand by the door and flung open the door of the sitting-room.

Sir Charles Fraith was curled up asleep on the sofa, the cats on his lap. 'How the hell did you get in here?' howled Agatha.

He opened his eyes and smiled and stretched with the same lazy insolence as her cats, who both slinked down from the sofa to wind themselves around her legs. 'Don't you remember, Aggie? I have a set of keys. You gave them to me ages ago. You do look ferocious.'

'Where's your car? I didn't see it.'

'Down the lane at the end.'

Agatha sank down in a chair and surveyed him. 'You nearly frightened me to death. You look . . . different.'

The pompous married Charles she had last seen, fat with thinning hair, had disappeared. In his place was the old Charles, neat, slim and impeccably tailored and with a full head of hair.

'Have you had a hair weave?'

'No, I got over the cancer. The chemotherapy was making it fall out.'

'Cancer!' squeaked Agatha in horror. She remembered when James had had cancer and had not told her and her heart gave a lurch. 'You didn't tell me!'

'Didn't tell most people. They all begin to act funny.'

'Cancer of what?'

'The lung.'

'Blimey!'

'Yes, blimey. But I'm cured and as fit as a fiddle.'

'How's the wife and children?'

'Can I have a drink?'

Agatha stood up and went over to the drinks cupboard, saying over her shoulder, 'Not like you not to help yourself.'

'I meant to. But after I had read the local papers I fell asleep. Scotch, Aggie, a malt if you've got it.'

Agatha poured him a generous measure and then one for herself.

'Cheers,' she said, sitting down. 'You haven't answered my question. How's the family?'

'Gone. All gone.'

'What happened?'

'While I was in hospital, she nipped back to Paris and fell in love with someone twenty years younger. He's French, rich, well-connected. Her family forked out a fortune for the divorce.'

'How dreadful! Your children! How you must miss them!'

He took a sip of his drink. 'I have visiting rights and they can come and stay with Papa any time they want. I doubt if they will. Like a couple of little aliens. Very dark and French. Wouldn't speak English.'

'You must have felt shattered.'

He looked amused. 'On the contrary, I thought I was blessed. No more cancer, no more nagging French wife. Goodbye to both.'

Agatha surveyed him curiously. 'People who recover from cancer are usually very spiritual. I mean, they feel they have been given a second chance at life, sort of born again.'

Charles looked amused. 'Do they? How odd.'

Selfish and self-centred and self-contained as ever, thought Agatha.

'So what brings you?'

'A mixture of curiosity and boredom. My aunt has turned the whole house over to some fund-raising gala for the Red Cross. I've got to get out of this, I thought. There's murder and mayhem been going on over in Aggie's direction, and I bet myself you were in the thick of it.'

'I wish I weren't,' said Agatha. 'I'll tell you about it. But first, do you mind if I go upstairs and put on something more comfortable?'

'Not at all.' His eyes gleamed with mischief. 'I thought you would never ask.'

Agatha went upstairs and put on a black-and-gold caftan she had bought years ago in

Turkey and changed out of her high heels and put on slippers. It was nice to see Charles, she reflected. She wouldn't have to bother about her appearance.

She went back downstairs and called to her cats, filled up their food bowls with some fish she had poached before she left and then opened the garden door so that they could get out after they had finished eating.

Outside, at the end of Lilac Lane, Mrs Davenport walked away. Agatha had re-entered the living-room and drawn back the curtains. Earlier, Mrs Davenport had seen a man let himself in. In her handbag, she had Juanita's address. She had got it by being in the general stores at just the right time. It had transpired that Juanita was extremely fond of the local fudge and had written to order a box of it. 'I'll send her one as well,' Mrs Davenport had said. 'I had her address but I've lost it.' Having secured the address, she had written a letter to Juanita to inform her that her husband was having an affair with Agatha Raisin. She did not sign it. No reason to let the formidable Mrs Raisin know that she was the one who had informed on her.

Agatha sat down. 'That's better,' she said. 'I like the curtains open when I'm at home. I only close them when I go to bed.'

'So tell me all about it,' said Charles.

Agatha began at the beginning and went on to the end, soothed by Charles's capacity for listening.

'What a mess,' he commented when she had finished. 'Before I give you my views, what about Paul? Am I interfering in your love life?'

'He's married. Anyway, how could you interfere?'

'I took the liberty of unpacking my things in the spare room.'

'You do assume a lot, you cheeky sod. All right, you can stay. So what do you think of the murders? I cannot believe for a moment this Harry Witherspoon is the murderer.'

'Why? He's the only one who stood to gain from her death.'

'I know, I know. I can imagine him doing the first one but not the second. He and his sister asked Paul and me to find the murderer of their mother.'

'You left that bit out.'

'Sorry.'

'I'd like to meet him.'

'I'm sure he's been with the police for a long time. We could try tomorrow. It would be only polite to tell Paul and see if he wants to go with us.'

There was a sharp ring at the doorbell.

'It's a bit late for anyone to be calling,' said Agatha, getting to her feet. 'Hope it's not that awful Runcorn. I don't feel up to him tonight.'

She opened the door. Paul stood there. 'I saw your car,' he said.

'Come in,' said Agatha. 'I've got a friend here.'

She led the way into the living-room and introduced Charles. 'Charles helped me on a lot of previous cases,' said Agatha.

'We thought we'd go and see Harry Witherspoon tomorrow,' said Charles. He yawned and stretched. 'You tell him about it, Aggie. I'm off to bed.' He walked towards the door and then turned and smiled at Agatha. 'Don't be long, dear,' he said.

There was an awkward silence.

Then Agatha said, 'It's not what you think. Charles is just a friend.'

'A pretty intimate one, it seems to me,' said Paul. 'I'd better go.'

'Don't you want to come with us to see Harry tomorrow?'

'No, I'll be off. Three's a crowd.'

'Oh, don't be so silly. I'll send Charles away.'

'No need for that. I've got work to do anyway.' Paul left, looking decidedly huffy.

He returned to his own cottage. Two of the ladies of the village who had tried to court his company when he had first arrived had warned him about Agatha Raisin. They had hinted she'd had affairs. This had intrigued him and it was what had prompted him to approach Agatha in the first place. He had been quite disappointed at first to find himself faced with, not a femme fatale, but a prickly middle-aged woman. After he had got to know Agatha, he had admitted to himself that there was something very sexy about her, but the fact that he sensed the vulnerability under the hard shell had kept him from making any serious advances to her. He suddenly missed his volatile wife. He reached out for the phone and then decided against it. She would say the usual thing – if he loved her he would live in Spain – and they would end up having a row.

He did not feel sleepy. He switched on his computer. He would type out everything they had found out about the case and see if he could find a lead. It would be nice if he could solve the murders himself.

Agatha marched into the spare bedroom where Charles was lying, reading. 'Did you have to go and imply we were having an affair?' she demanded.

'Bit of fun, Aggie. Anyway, he shouldn't be sniffing around. You said your Watson was married.'

'He's not all that married,' said Agatha sulkily.

'Married is married. Anyway, he's a geek. A handsome one, I grant you, but a geek all the same. Not much personality.'

'Jealous, Charles?'

'Me! Never. Come and join me.'

'Don't you ever give up?'

'Worth a try,' said Charles, stretching lazily.

Agatha went out and banged the door.

She awoke early next morning to the smell of

frying bacon. She rose and washed and dressed and went down to the kitchen. 'I was just about to call you,' said Charles, standing at the stove. 'Breakfast's nearly ready.'

'Do make yourself free with my groceries,' said Agatha.

'I have done. One egg or two?'

'One.'

'I don't usually have breakfast, as you know,' said Agatha, sitting down at the table. 'I usually just have a cup of coffee.'

'This'll do you good.' He slid a plate of sausage, bacon and egg in front of her.

'I feel guilty about Paul,' said Agatha, poking at her food. When Charles turned back to the stove, she lifted a rasher of bacon and dropped it down on the floor for her cats to eat.

Charles helped himself to a plate of food and sat down opposite her. He was wearing casual dress – casual for him – a checked blue-and-white shirt with dark blue chinos.

'What I cannot understand,' he said between bites of food, 'is why the unfortunate Robin was killed and not you. You've been poking around asking questions about the murder and so far you haven't been threatened.'

'All it means is that she was close to something I missed.'

'I wonder what that could be? I'd like to meet this rector at Wormstone. Ask him a few more questions. There might have been something or someone she's been involved with. Did you ask him whether she had any relationships with men?'

'Don't think I did.'

'Well, there you are. Her murder might not have anything to do with this first one.' Charles finished his breakfast and stood up. Hodge, the cat, slid past him out into the garden, followed by Boswell. Hodge was holding a sausage in his mouth.

'Waste of food,' said Charles crossly. 'After all my hard work you're not supposed to feed your breakfast to the cats. So let's go.'

Harry Witherspoon's shop was closed and there was a FOR SALE sign in the window. 'Hope he's at home,' said Agatha. 'It's not far from here.'

Harry answered the door to them, blinking in the sunlight. 'Oh, it's you,' he said ungraciously. 'Come in. Who's this? Where's the other fellow?'

'This is Sir Charles Fraith, who has helped me on cases before.' Oh, the magic of a title, thought Agatha, as Harry smiled and began to fuss.

'Must offer you something. Too early for a drink?'

'Nothing for us,' said Agatha firmly. 'What about this Robin Barley business?'

'I can't understand it,' said Harry, looking bewildered. 'She was an infuriating woman. But to kill her, and in such an elaborate way!'

'And you weren't at the theatre?' asked Charles.

'No, thank God. At the time she was being murdered I was over in Broadway in a pub having drinks with this chap in the antiques business who is going to offer a good sum for my stock and may take over the shop as well. I need some ready cash. The lawyers say they can advance me money on Mother's will because I haven't been charged with anything, but I want to have the whole thing settled.'

'Did Robin have any lovers?' asked Agatha.

'I don't know. She went around in the company of a lot of young gays. Then she was friendly with her local rector. We all rather kept clear of her.'

'I want to ask you about that secret passage,' said Agatha. 'When Paul and I wanted to search the house, you refused permission. Why? Did you know about the passage?'

He shook his head. 'You've no idea what our upbringing was like. After school we were sent up to our rooms and locked in, only to be let out for half an hour for supper and then locked in for the night. I often climbed out of the window and escaped, just to get away. Mother found out and said Carol had told her. When I got into trouble, she always said it was Carol who had told her. Now, I see it was never Carol, it was just her way of divide and rule.'

'But your mother must have known about the passage.'

'I don't think so. I mean, when that ghost business started, if she'd known, she would have told the police. I know she once told me that when she'd bought the house there was a lot of old junk left in the cellar and she should really get someone to take it off to the tip. But she was penny-pinching, so I guess that was why she left it there.'

'I wonder if the two murders are connected,' said Charles.

'I can't see that they are.' Harry gave a weary shrug. 'Mind you, Robin infuriated a lot of people.'

'Not much there,' said Charles, as they drove towards the village of Wormstone. 'Let's hope the rector, Mr Potter, can come up with something.'

Mr Potter was welcoming but puzzled to find that Agatha should think he had anything to add to what he had already told her.

His housekeeper served them tea in the rectory garden, a peaceful place with apricot trees growing against a mellow stone wall and a large round pond where water-lilies opened their waxy petals to the sun. Agatha, looking at Mr Potter's mild, tranquil face and then round his peaceful garden, experienced a pang of envy. How pleasant it would be to be comfortable in one's own skin, to be free of worries and inadequacies.

Charles said, 'Perhaps there might be a clue in any relationships Mrs Barley might have had?'

'I don't really know of any. She was always busy. You would have thought her art and the theatre would take up all of her time, but she was always organizing something new.'

'Like what?' asked Agatha.

'Oh, so many things. Plays in the church. The village fête – provided she opened it. She had boundless energy.' His face suddenly creased in a smile. 'I thought she was going to be killed once.'

Agatha, who had been lounging in her chair, sat up straight. 'Tell us about it.'

'She had been over at Stow once, where the Sealed Knot were re-enacting the Battle of Worcester. Mrs Barley decided we were going to outdo the Sealed Knot in a re-enactment. She divided up the villagers into Roundheads and Cavaliers. It was that very hot summer a few years ago. I tried to point out to her that this is a very small village and we hadn't really enough people to play the parts, but she was determined because she said Midlands Television was going to film it. As I said, it was a very hot summer and she had made the mistake of supplying the "troops" with a plentiful amount of mead and cider. Instead of making everyone cheerful, the drink made a lot of people tetchy, and what with the heat and a general dislike of being bullied into things by Mrs Barley, tempers began to run high. We had to wait about because no television

216

camera appeared. At last, she shouted to them to go ahead, and the battle began to get nasty. I said to her I was frightened someone would get hurt.

'She strode into the midst of the battle, shouting, "Stop it! You are behaving like children." She jumped back to avoid being trampled by a horse, tripped and sat down on a cow-pat. The whole crowd erupted into laughter. It was very cruel of the villagers, but it restored good humour. Poor Mrs Barley just walked away. Her face was scarlet and she was nearly in tears.'

'She would need advice to get it right,' said Agatha slowly. 'Did she have some sort of historical expert to help her?'

'Mrs Barley might have had. But if she had, she didn't tell me.'

'But don't you think,' said Agatha eagerly, 'that she might have asked for expert advice? Have you heard of a Mr Peter Frampton?'

'No. You see, a lot of people came and went in Mrs Barley's life.'

'Thank you for the tea,' said Agatha, getting to her feet. 'There's someone I've got to see.'

'Peter Frampton?' asked Charles. 'Who's he? You didn't mention him.'

'He heads a historical society at Towdey, which is a village near Hebberdon. Paul and I went to one of his lectures. It was supposed to be on local history, but we got a lecture on the

Battle of Worcester instead. There was something else odd. This young girl, Zena Saxon, turned up during the lecture. I think she and Frampton are an item, which is odd.'

'Why?'

'Well, I would guess she's in her early twenties, sort of local disco chick, and he's in his late forties – grey hair, stylish, looks like a Conservative MP out of central casting.'

'Why on earth would he murder anyone?'

'He wanted Ivy Cottage, Mrs Witherspoon's house. Maybe he thought he could find the treasure. Maybe he knew about the secret passage.'

'What does he do when he's not giving historical lectures?'

'I don't know. That's what we're going to Hebberdon to find out.'

They were driving through Mircester when Agatha cried, 'Stop the car!'

Charles swerved in towards the kerb and parked on a double yellow line. 'Be quick,' he urged. 'I don't want to get a ticket for illegal parking. What is it?'

'I just saw Paul going into a pub with Haley.'

'And who's Haley?' asked Charles patiently.

'She's a policewoman. Bill's quite keen on her. Paul offered to give her computer lessons.'

'So that explains what he's doing.'

'He could be finding out things about the case from her.'

'If he finds out anything, I'm sure he'll let you know.'

Agatha hardly ever recognized feelings of jealousy in herself. She persuaded herself that it was in the interests of the case to find out what Paul was doing.

'I'll just go and join them,' she said.

'I can't wait here!' complained Charles. 'I'll get booked.'

'Then find somewhere legal to park and join us.'

Agatha got out of the car and hurried off in the direction of the pub.

Paul and Haley were sitting at a corner table when she walked in. 'Hello!' said Agatha with a crocodile smile that contained no humour whatsoever.

Paul looked at her with an expression of dismay on his face. Agatha thought sourly he looked like an adulterous husband caught in the act.

'What are you doing here, Agatha?' he asked.

'I saw you and Haley and thought I'd join you,' said Agatha, preparing to sit down.

'Do you mind not joining us, Agatha? I'm going to talk computer stuff with Haley and I'm sure you'd find it very boring.'

'Oh, in that case . . .' Agatha turned towards the door.

'I'll talk to you later,' he called.

Agatha went out and looked up and down the street. Charles was still parked where she had left him.

'You didn't find a legal parking place?' asked Agatha, sliding into the passenger seat.

'Didn't even try. I felt in my bones you wouldn't be long.'

'Why?'

'When a middle-aged gent goes into a pub with a saucy blonde, I don't think he wants anyone butting in.'

'It's not like that,' said Agatha. 'I met her with Bill and she asked Paul to help her with some computer stuff.'

'And so kindly helpful Paul sends you off with a flea in your ear?'

'I'm sure he'll explain it all later,' said Agatha huffily.

'And look at it his way. He finds you cosy with me and gets jealous.'

'He wouldn't have been jealous if you hadn't implied we were having an affair!'

'You should be grateful to me,' said Charles loftily. 'Nothing like a bit of competition to spice things up a bit. You never talk about James.'

'Leave it.'

'Okay.'

'This is an odd village,' said Charles as he parked in Towdey's main street. 'All these little thatched cottages crouched along the road like so many animals. Secretive-looking place.'

'It's getting dark,' said Agatha, ever practical. 'I think it's going to rain.'

They rang the doorbell of Frampton's cottage, but there was no reply.

220

'I suppose he must be out working at something,' said Agatha. 'There's a general store along the street. We'll try there.'

A woman behind the shop counter told them that Mr Frampton owned a building and demolition works in the new industrial estate outside Moreton-in-Marsh.

'So that's where he gets his money from,' said Agatha as they got back into the car. 'I wonder if that sort of demolition work means he could get his hands on cyanide.'

'Shouldn't think so. I know cyanide is used in mining. We'll see what he has to say for himself.'

'Have you any cards on you?' asked Agatha.

'Yes, why?'

'I think he's a snob and I'm hoping to melt him with your title.'

'You're an old-fashioned girl, Aggie. I'm a mere baronet, not a duke. And a title doesn't melt anyone these days with so many odds and sods in the House of Lords.'

'Let's see anyway.'

'Where is this industrial estate?'

'Turn off on the Oxford road. It's just a few miles out of town.'

Frampton's Building Works was a large, prosperous-looking modern building. And inside a glittering reception area which seemed to have been fashioned out of steel tubes and then decorated with plants sat Zena Saxon behind a desk. She had toned down her dress and make-up for work, or so it seemed. She was wearing a neat white blouse and subdued make-up, but when she stood up to greet them and walked round the desk, she revealed that on the lower half of her body she was wearing brief sky-blue shorts and very high stilettos.

'Wow!' whispered Charles.

He presented his card, introduced Agatha, and asked if they could speak to Peter Frampton.

'What about? I think he's busy right now,' said Zena. She had a nasal singsong Birmingham accent.

'Please ask,' urged Charles.

She shrugged. 'Wait here.' She swayed off into the nether regions.

'Frampton's a lucky man,' said Charles. 'That must be the best bum in the Midlands.'

'Control yourself,' snapped Agatha, reflecting moodily on the plight of middle-aged women who had to watch equally middle-aged men lusting after girls young enough to be their daughters.

She was gone quite a long time but eventually reappeared, followed by Peter Frampton, impeccably tailored and carrying a hard hat in one hand.

'Is this important?' he asked.

'It is,' said Charles. 'Did you know a Mrs Robin Barley?'

Frampton frowned. He pressed one long finger

222

against his forehead. Then his face cleared. 'Can't say I do.'

'You don't seem surprised at the question,' said Agatha.

'Should I be?'

'Mrs Robin Barley is the woman who has just been so dramatically murdered with cyanide.'

'Oh, *that* Mrs Robin Barley. That's why the name sounded familiar and gave me pause. But, no, sorry.'

'But the rector of Wormstone said you were advising her on the historical details of the Battle of Worcester, which was being re-enacted in the village,' lied Agatha.

'Was I? Dear me, when was this?'

'I'm not quite sure,' said Agatha, wishing in that moment she'd asked the rector when the village Battle of Worcester had taken place.

He shook his handsome head. 'I can't help you, I'm afraid. I meet a lot of people.'

'Why did you ask Mrs Witherspoon to sell her house to you?' asked Charles.

'It's an interesting building and my passion is the seventeenth century.'

'But it's a Tudor house, isn't it?'

'I am fascinated with old buildings, that's all.'

'I asked you this before,' said Agatha, 'but I'll ask you again. Did you hope to find Sir Geoffrey Lamont's treasure?'

'I am sure that is long gone and I am sure previous owners of Ivy Cottage searched the place from the cellar to the rafters.'

'But why do you want to move into such a large house?' pursued Agatha.

'Meaning a single man should not want space? My dear Mrs Raisin, I have an extensive library of historical books, some of them valuable and quite a lot in storage because at the moment I do not have room for them. Now if you don't mind, I have work to do.'

They reluctantly left, unable to think of any more questions.

When they got back to Agatha's cottage, Paul ran along to meet them. 'The case is over,' he said. 'Harry's been arrested.'

'Why? How?' asked Agatha.

'He was over at Hebberdon around the time of the murder. The landlord of the local pub in Hebberdon saw him and was blackmailing him. Harry cracked and went to the police. He was seen going up to the house just before eleven o'clock at night.'

'But surely the cast said he was at the party after the show?' exclaimed Agatha.

'Well, you can't imagine someone like Harry being the life and soul of the party. He could easily slip away and come back without anyone noticing.'

'I suppose the landlord's been arrested,' said Charles.

'They're looking for him. He's disappeared.'

'I suppose you got all this out of Haley,' said Agatha.

'Yes, she was very excited about it all.'

Agatha hesitated and then said, 'Let's all go inside.'

Paul looked at Charles and shrugged. 'I'll leave you to it. I've got work to do.'

'I thought you were taking a break.' Agatha looked at him pleadingly.

'Can't afford to always be on holiday. See you around.'

He walked away.

'He would have stayed if you hadn't been here,' said Agatha sulkily.

'He's married, Aggie. No hope there.'

'How do you know that?' howled Agatha. 'His wife's in Spain. His marriage is on the rocks.'

Mrs Davenport, idling on the other side of the lane with her dog, listened avidly.

Agatha suddenly saw her and dragged Charles inside. 'That awful woman,' she said. 'She always seems to be snooping around.'

'Same could be said for you, Aggie. Like a drink?'

'No. I think I'd like to go and see Bill. I don't believe it's Harry.'

'If it's not Harry, why didn't he tell the police he was there?'

'He may have found her dead.'

'He didn't have a key. Maybe he just knocked at the door and getting no answer, went back to the party. When he heard she'd been found murdered, he panicked.'

'Maybe, maybe, maybe. I'm going to phone Mircester and see if Bill's there.'

'Suit yourself. I'm having a drink.'

Agatha phoned and then joined Charles in the sitting-room. He sat cradling a large whisky and with the cats on his lap.

'Bill's gone home,' said Agatha. 'I'm going over to see him. Coming?'

'If I must. Wait till I finish this drink.'

'No!'

'Okay, I'll take it with me. You drive.'

Fortunately for both of them, it was Bill himself who answered the door and not one of his formidable parents. 'Come in,' he said. 'My parents are out. It's their bingo night.'

'We hear Harry's been arrested and that landlord was blackmailing him and now he's gone missing and I don't think it's Harry and there's been some terrible mistake . . .'

'Whoa, Agatha! Hold your horses. Who told you? Nothing's been issued to the press.'

Agatha suddenly did not want to tell him about Haley, in case he was hurt, in case Paul got into trouble. 'We have our sources,' she said.

'Sit down,' said Bill, his face impassive. 'That friend of yours, Paul Chatterton, took Haley for lunch.'

'Oh, Bill, does it really matter how we know? What do you think about it?'

'It's all circumstantial evidence. There's no forensic evidence and the one witness who says Harry was there has disappeared. But Harry does inherit a lot of money and he lied to the police. Mrs Barley was asking around about where he was during the evening and suddenly she's murdered. Runcorn is determined it is Harry and he's holding a press conference tomorrow. Mrs Barley had been phoning various members of the cast.

'We've checked her phone calls. She must have made about twenty calls. And look at it this way. If it's not Harry, then who else could it possibly be?'

'Sister Carol?'

'I don't see the sister having the strength or the expertise to deliver a blow like the one that killed Mrs Witherspoon. Furthermore Harry says he did not take part in the production of *Macbeth* because of his hay fever. And yet there were no hay fever treatments at his house.'

'If it was just the death of his mother, I might, I just might think it was Harry,' said Agatha. 'But all that business with cyanide! It just doesn't make sense.'

'If we ever find Barry Briar, that landlord, then we might have a clearer idea.'

'I suppose the police are looking for him everywhere?'

'Of course.'

'I can't believe in the fact that if Harry is innocent, he has nothing to fear,' said Agatha. 'Not with a twit like Runcorn running things.'

'Runcorn put your back up, Agatha. He may have an abrasive manner, but he's a conscientious policeman.'

Agatha muttered something that sounded like *pah*.

'I haven't offered you anything to drink,' said Bill. 'Would you like some sherry?'

'No, thanks,' said Charles and Agatha together, knowing by experience that the brand of sweet sherry, the only drink the Wongs kept for visitors, was vile.

'The only advice I can give you,' said Bill, 'is the advice I gave you before. Keep out of it. If it's not Harry, then for the moment the murderer will believe himself safe. If you keep poking around, you could be in danger. Where's Paul, or has Charles's presence driven him away?'

'Not at all. He thinks it's all over and has gone back to work.'

'How is your wife, Charles?'

'Ex.'

'Ah. There's nothing more I can help you with.'

Agatha and Charles went to dinner in Mircester. To Agatha's amazement, Charles paid. As Agatha drove them home, she said, 'Planning on staying with me for a bit?'

'Why not? Paul's a non-starter, Aggie. You

228

have a genius for chasing after men who are going to hurt you.'

'I wasn't thinking about Paul,' lied Agatha, who had been thinking about him on and off all evening.

'Anyway, let's get a good night's sleep and maybe go over to Hebberdon in the morning and ferret around.'

After she fell asleep, Agatha had a nightmare in which she was meticulously scrubbing and cleaning the secret passage. Thick cobwebs brushed her face and she clawed them away. She felt she should not go on because there was something terrible awaiting her at the end of the passage. She awoke with a start and lay there with her heart thudding. What a horrible dream. She stared up at the beamed ceiling wondering where the landlord, Barry Briar, had got to. Then she wondered why whoever had killed Mrs Witherspoon, because she still could not believe the murderer to be Harry, had not just put her body down into the secret passage. It could have lain there, undiscovered, for ages. Marvellous place to hide a body.

She sat up straight. What if the murderer had killed Barry? If he had been blackmailing Harry, then why not someone else?

Would the police think of searching for a *body*? What better place to dump a body than down in the secret passage in a house that had already been gone over thoroughly by the police?

She got out of bed and went through to the spare bedroom and shook Charles awake. He switched on the bedside light and surveyed the glory of Agatha Raisin in a diaphanous black nightie which she had recently bought without admitting to herself that she hoped Paul might see her in it.

'Why, Aggie,' said Charles with a grin. 'Welcome! Come and join me.'

'Charles! Listen! I think the landlord's body might be down in that secret passage.'

'So? Phone Bill in the morning and put it to him.'

'No, I want to go now and look.'

Charles yawned. 'Good hunting!'

'You are coming with me!'

'Oh, Aggie.' He twisted his head and looked at the bedside clock. 'It's three in the bloody morning.'

'Please.'

'Oh, very well.' He threw back the blankets and eased his naked body out of bed. He stretched and walked over and stared out of the open window. Mrs Davenport drew back into the shrubbery across the road, gazing avidly at the lamplit tableau under the thatched roof. Agatha Raisin in a see-through black nightie. She could not see Charles's head because the low window only afforded her a view of his naked torso.

As Charles turned away, Mrs Davenport

scuttled off down the lane, her conscience eased. After she had written to Juanita, she had been frightened that she had exaggerated. But now she had just seen proof positive of Agatha's affair with Paul. She was so determined to find Agatha guilty that she discounted the fact that Charles was staying with Agatha. Charles, she decided, must have left. Hadn't Mrs Bloxby told her the other day that Sir Charles Fraith was simply an old friend?

If she had waited, she would have seen Charles and Agatha emerge from the house and drive off.

'All this because you had a nightmare,' grumbled Charles. 'I assume we can get to the damned passage from the garden. I don't feel like housebreaking.'

'Yes, we can. I hope the police haven't sealed off the trapdoor.'

'No reason why they should. It's not their property.'

'Drive right up to the house,' ordered Agatha. 'I don't care if anyone sees us.'

'We're trespassing, even if it is only the garden.'

'Harry's the owner and I've got his permission to investigate the case. That's what I'll say if we're caught. Turn up here.'

'It's certainly isolated,' said Charles, switching

off the engine. 'I wonder what the landlord was doing skulking around.'

'Let's go and get it over with.' Agatha got out of the car. The night was very still. A small moon riding overhead silvered a mackerel sky and a breeze sent the ivy which covered the old cottage rippling and whispering.

'Creepy,' muttered Charles. 'Are you really sure you want to go through with this?'

'May as well. We're here now. Better put our gloves on.' They made their way round the side of the house and into the garden. 'Right down at the end,' said Agatha. 'It's in that clump of shrubbery.'

An owl sailed overhead, making them jump. They crept into the shrubbery. Agatha took out a small torch and shone it on the ground.

'There's the trapdoor,' she said.

'If we have to go down there, we'll leave foot-prints,' cautioned Charles.

'So? I mean, if there's no body, we don't have to worry.'

Charles heaved open the trapdoor. 'Shine the torch down,' said Charles. 'It's so dark I can't even see the stairs.'

Agatha shone the thin beam of the torch down the stairs, let out a squawk and dropped the torch and clutched at Charles so hard he fell back with a crash into the bushes.

'Aggie,' he complained. 'What the hell . . .?'

'Eyes,' stammered Agatha. 'Eyes. Down there.'

'Where's the damned torch?' demanded

Charles, struggling to his feet. He felt around the ground until he located it.

'Get out of my way and I'll have a look.'

Charles shone the torch down. He gave a muttered exclamation and went down a few steps. Then he retreated back up.

'It's a dead body.'

'Is it Barry Briar?'

'I don't know. Never met the man. Have a look.'

'No, I think I'm going to be sick.'

'Leave everything as it is. I'm calling the police.'

'Must we? I mean, they'll be awfully angry.'

'Aggie, someone's dead down there. We can't just walk away.'

'How do you know he's dead?'

'If a man's lying with his neck twisted and his lifeless eyes glaring up at you, it's ten to one he's dead. Let's get out of this shrubbery.'

They emerged into the garden and sat down on the grass. Charles took out his mobile phone and called the police while Agatha hugged her knees and shivered.

'Gloves,' she said when Charles rang off. 'It looks criminal, us wearing gloves.'

'I'm not going back there to put fingerprints on the trapdoor. I am wearing an ordinary pair of gloves. Sort of thing a man would wear to lift a dirty trapdoor lid. Stop worrying.'

'They'll wonder how I knew where the entrance was.'

'It said in the newspapers that a secret passage led from the house to the garden. You had this brainwave, so we searched the garden and found it. Don't you want to go back and have a peek and make sure it's the missing landlord?'

'I can't.'

'Well, we'll soon know. You're getting soft in the country, Aggie. I'm sure the city mouse wouldn't be in such a shake.'

'Charles, I've often wondered if you've any feelings at all.'

'Oh, lots and lots. But I didn't know this landlord and he sounds no end of a creep. I can hear sirens. Won't be long. I'd better get my lawyer out of bed.'

'Why? We didn't murder him.'

'Try telling Runcorn that. "Oh, officer," says Aggie, "I had a dream." He's not going to buy that.'

It was a long night. Agatha and Charles and Charles's sleepy lawyer waited and waited after being taken to police headquarters for their interviews.

Agatha was to be interviewed first. At last she was summoned and the lawyer rose to join her.

The lawyer, a Mr Jellicoe, was an imposing figure and Agatha was sure that without his steely interruptions, Runcorn would have grilled her to the point where she would almost feel like

234

confessing to murder just to have the interview over.

Then it was Charles's turn.

The noon sunshine was streaming in through the dusty windows of police headquarters when he came out to join her. 'They're giving us a lift back to Hebberdon.' They both thanked the lawyer and went out to where the police car was waiting. Haley was at the wheel.

'Oh, it's you,' said Agatha, sliding into the back seat with Charles.

'How's Paul?' asked Haley as she drove off.

'Fine,' said Agatha. 'I gather from the horrible Runcorn that the body we found was the landlord's.'

'I'm not allowed to discuss the case.'

'Oh, really?' snapped Agatha. 'Then how come you flapped your mouth off to Paul?'

The back of Haley's neck turned pink. 'That was private.'

'Aggie,' said Charles warningly, 'we're too tired for a fight.'

Agatha relapsed into a resentful silence, only waking when Haley drew up at Ivy Cottage.

'Thank you,' said Charles politely and Haley flashed him a smile.

'Trollop,' muttered Agatha as they walked to their car.

'Now, Aggie, that's nothing but jealousy.'

Agatha ignored the remark and slid into the passenger seat. 'God, I'm tired. I only hope for Harry's sake that the police find some evidence that Barry Briar was blackmailing someone else.'

'We'll sleep on it.'

Back at her cottage, Agatha switched off the phone and disconnected the doorbell. 'Don't want to be disturbed,' she said. 'I'm going to sleep as long as possible.'

'I'm going to make breakfast.'

'Help yourself. I'm too tired to eat.'

Before Agatha plunged down into sleep, she wondered what Paul would make of the latest development and wished that Charles would take himself off.

Chapter Ten

Agatha's first thought on waking later in the day was that they should try to see Carol and then go on to Wormstone. When she got up, it was to find Charles was still asleep. She defrosted a package which turned out to be lasagne, micro-waved it and ate it. Then she phoned Paul but didn't get a reply.

Impatient for action, she woke Charles and then had a shower and dressed. Charles was in the kitchen when she went downstairs, playing with the cats by tossing a crumpled ball of aluminium foil in the air and watching them leap for it.

She surveyed the scene from the kitchen door, wondering, as she had wondered so many times in the past, what Charles really thought about her. He came and went at will, always as self-contained and enigmatic as her cats.

'I thought we should try to see Carol and find out how Harry's getting on and then go to Wormstone,' she said.

'Righto,' said Charles lazily. He opened the

kitchen bin to drop the foil into it and looked down at the discarded package of lasagne. 'Aggie, you're supposed to eat a certain amount of fresh fruit and vegetables each day. All you do is smoke, drink black coffee, and eat trash. You'll get spots.'

'I'm too old to get spots.'

'One is never too old to get spots. Or cancer.'

'I haven't had cancer. You've had cancer.'

'But I swear it's my healthy life-style that fought it off. Okay, let's go.'

Carol was at home. Her eyes were blotchy with recently shed tears. 'Poor Harry,' she said. 'Isn't it awful?'

'He has been actually charged, has he?' asked Charles.

'They've charged him with the murder of Mother. Oh, dear, what can I do?'

'We're working on it,' said Agatha. 'Did he say why he went over to see your mother that particular night?'

'He said he couldn't stop worrying about the financial mess he was in. He said it was just an impulse. He wanted to try again to see if she would lend him some money. He said he got no reply. He assumed she had seen him from the window and had decided not to open the door. She had done that before. So he just drove back and joined the party.'

'It's a wonder the stage-door man didn't see him coming and going.'

'Freddy was at the party himself. They decided there was no need for him to man the stage door after the party began.'

'Are you sure neither of you knew about that secret passage?'

'Quite sure.'

'Then why were you both so reluctant to let us search the house?'

'Harry had been down in the cellar and he said there was a lot of stuff there, old toys, things like that. He said we might be able to get a good price for some of it.' She turned pink. 'He was worried you might pinch some of it.'

Agatha experienced a flash of dislike for Harry. He probably did the murders, she thought.

'Had he paid Barry any money?' asked Charles.

'No. But he promised to. He said he would pay him when he got his inheritance.'

'How much was Barry asking for?'

'Fifty thousand pounds.'

'I wonder when Barry was murdered,' said Agatha. 'You see, if it turns out he was murdered while Harry was in jail, then surely the police will have to let him go. Because that would prove that Barry was probably blackmailing someone else.'

A gleam of hope lit up Carol's watery eyes. 'Can you find out?'

'I'll try,' said Agatha, thinking of Bill Wong.

'Now, why Wormstone?' asked Charles as they got back into the car.

'I don't like Peter Frampton.'

'So why don't we go and spit in his face? He's in Towdey, not Wormstone.'

'Because it's a long shot. What if Robin Barley asked him for advice on the Civil War?'

'The rector couldn't remember.'

'But someone in the village might. We won't take long.'

Paul Chatterton was at that moment in Towdey, looking for Zena Saxton's address. He had typed notes into his computer of all he and Agatha had found out. He had more or less made up his mind that Harry had actually committed the murders, but he felt that Peter Frampton was a loose end to be tied up. He had wanted Ivy Cottage. Why that particular cottage? He was cross with Agatha because she was neglecting him in favour of Charles.

He knocked at the door of the first house in the village he came to and was told that Zena lived in a cottage near the church, Dove Cottage.

Paul was relieved to see lights were on in the cottage. He hoped Peter Frampton wasn't with Zena.

Zena opened the door to him. Paul introduced

himself and said he had seen her briefly at the historical society. She looked at him with stony eyes. 'You're another of those snoops. What do you want?'

Paul smiled. 'As a matter of fact, I wanted to take you out for dinner.'

Vanity warred with suspicion in Zena's beautiful face. She was only wearing light make-up and a simple black sheath and Paul reflected that she was incredibly attractive and knew it.

Vanity obviously won. 'I'd like to,' she said cautiously, 'but my boyfriend said he might call round.'

'Keep him guessing,' said Paul. He was wearing his best suit and shirt and a silk tie.

'Where did you think of taking me for dinner?' asked Zena.

'Le Beau Gentilhomme.'

'Oh, I'll get my bag,' said Zena. 'I've always wanted to go there but my boyfriend says it's too expensive.'

When she went indoors to collect her handbag, Paul thanked his stars that Peter Frampton should prove to be a cheapskate. Le Beau Gentilhomme was a new French restaurant in Mircester.

'Well, here's Wormstone,' said Charles. 'Where do we start?'

'There's the Black Bear pub over there. We'll try there first.'

The pub was crowded. Agatha bought them both drinks at the bar. Charles, obviously regretting his earlier generosity in buying her a meal, said he couldn't find his wallet.

Agatha was suddenly reluctant to waylay some local and start asking questions. I am getting soft, she thought.

'Let's start with that old codger over in the corner,' suggested Charles.

A gnarled gnome of a man sat nursing a pint of cider. 'Evening,' said Charles. 'Mind if we join you?'

The gnome raised his pint and drank it down to the dregs. 'I'd like another,' he said.

'Aggie, could you? I've . . .'

'Forgotten my wallet. I know.' Agatha went over to the bar and ordered another pint of cider for the old man.

When she rejoined him at the table, Charles said, 'This is Bert Smallbone. He was just telling me about the Battle of Worcester.'

'When was that?' asked Agatha.

'That'd be 1651.'

'No, I mean the re-enactment in the village.'

'The re what?'

'I mean the one you put on in the village.'

'Ur. I thought him –' he jerked a thumb at Charles – 'were asking 'bout the real one.'

'What we want to know is whether Mrs Robin Barley hired an expert – a historical expert – to advise her.'

'I dunno. Silly woman, she were. Allus prancing about shouting orders. I were a Cavalier.'

Charles reflected that no one had surely ever looked less like a Cavalier than Bert.

'But you don't know whether anyone was advising her or not?' asked Agatha impatiently.

He shook his head.

Agatha had had enough. She half-rose. 'Thank you for your time, Mr Smallbone.'

'Reckon her didn't need no expert,' said Bert. 'Mrs Know-all. Her had battle plans, fair like blueprints o' house.'

Charles reached up a hand and pressed Agatha back into her seat. 'I don't suppose any of these plans are still around?'

Bert tilted back a greasy cap and scratched his head. 'Reckon not,' he said. 'Mrs Barley had 'em.'

'Oh, well,' said Charles, giving up. 'Thank you for your time.'

'We'd better try someone else,' said Agatha as they walked towards the bar.

'I don't think so. They are all men in here. We want a woman. A gossip.'

Charles leaned across the bar and said to the barman, 'Is there a woman in this village who knows everything that goes on in the village?'

He laughed. 'That 'ud be Jenny Feathers.'

'And where do we find her?'

'Five doors down to your left.'

'Thanks.'

'What are you after, Charles? About these

battle maps?' asked Agatha when they were outside.

'I thought if someone else had drawn them up, then there might be a name on them. Let's try this gossip.'

Jenny Feathers was a thin, energetic woman with greying hair and thick glasses. Agatha let Charles do the talking.

'Do come in,' she said. They followed her into a cluttered parlour. There were various arrangements of dried flowers and lots of little occasional tables covered with china ornaments and framed photographs.

'Do make yourselves comfortable.' Agatha and Charles sat side by side on a small chintz-covered sofa, so small that Agatha could feel Charles's hip pressing against her own.

Jenny sat on a tapestry-covered Victorian chair facing them. 'You were asking about our village performance of the Battle of Worcester? Such a shambles. My dears, I actually felt sorry for Robin when she fell on to that cow-pat. The day was so hot, you see, and she was apt to bully people. Not me, of course. I could put her in her place. But then it is always a matter of breeding, don't you think, Sir Charles? The locals are simple people.'

'We wondered if Robin Barley had consulted any sort of historical expert,' said Charles.

'Now, then, that I doubt, or if she did, she would never let on. She liked to pretend she knew everything.'

'But she had some sort of battle plans drawn up, did she not? We wondered if anyone would still have some of those.'

She shook her head. 'She had a couple, but she probably took them home. Poor woman. Such a sad death. But she was so annoying, you see.'

'Did she have any gentlemen friends?' asked Agatha.

'Oh, people came and went. We got so used to seeing strangers visiting her. That man the police are saying murdered her, he visited her once.'

Harry, thought Agatha. Another nail in his coffin.

'You didn't ever see her with a tall, handsome man – grey wavy hair?'

'I can't remember.' Jenny looked at Agatha with dislike. She prided herself on her knowledge of what went on in the village and did not like having to say that she knew so little of Robin Barley's private life.

'When was this mock battle?' asked Charles.

'That would be four summers ago.'

They thanked her and left.

'I think we're wasting time chasing after Peter Frampton,' said Charles. 'I mean, why murder three people and all over a house and a mythical treasure?'

'I don't know. Just a feeling. What time is it?'

'Just after nine. Why?'

'How long to Oxford?'

'I could make it in three quarters of an hour. Why?'

'There's someone I want to see.'

Paul was beginning to think that the prices in this pretentious restaurant were a waste of money, much as Zena appeared to be enjoying herself.

He was dismayed to find out that the boy-friend she had been talking about was not Peter Frampton, but some local youth who worked in a garage.

'I thought you and Peter Frampton were an item,' he said.

'My boss? Keep him sweet. He gives me presents. He thinks he's going to marry me.'

'And are you?'

'No, he's ever so old.' Paul reflected that Peter Frampton was probably at least a couple of years younger than himself.

'You see,' said Zena earnestly, 'I'm a bit of a women's libber.'

'No, I don't see. What's that got to do with it?'

'Well,' she said, leaning her elbows on the table, 'it's like this, see? Men have been exploiting women for centuries, so it's fair game to take them for what you can get.'

'Oh, really? And what do you get out of Peter?'

'Meals like this. Presents. He gave me a diamond necklace for Christmas.' She giggled. 'I told my boyfriend it was fake.'

'And what does Peter get in return?'

'Bit of slap and tickle. I tell him I'll go the whole way when we're married. Keep him guessing.'

'Peter Frampton seemed very keen to get his hands on Ivy Cottage.'

Was it a trick of the light or were her large eyes suddenly veiled?

'Oh, him, he's dotty about history. He hates all those history professors and so-called experts. He says he knows more about the seventeenth century and the Civil War than the lot of them. Tell you what, I'm bored stiff with history. When he's rabbiting on, I just think of something else.'

'Did he believe Sir Geoffrey Lamont's treasure was still hidden somewhere in Ivy Cottage?'

'Can I have a sweet?'

'Yes, of course.' Paul signalled for the menu.

He waited impatiently until she had made her choice and then asked again about the treasure.

'Look,' said Zena impatiently, 'if you want to know anything, ask Peter. You're beginning to bore me.'

'So who is this bod we're going to see?' asked Charles.

'Do you remember William Dalrymple?'

'No. Wait a bit. Wasn't he that history don?'

247

'That's the one. We met him when we were investigating Melissa's murder.'

'Ah, Melissa. The one James had a fling with before he disappeared.'

'I don't want to talk about that.'

'So why William Dalrymple?'

'I'm curious,' said Agatha. 'I want to know how passionate history buffs can get about their subject.'

'You're wondering if Frampton could get passionate enough to kill?'

'Yes.'

'Very far-fetched. Although I must admit I still cannot believe it was Harry who murdered Robin Barley. Of course, we may be dealing with two murderers.'

'Let's see what William has to say.'

William Dalrymple was at home. 'I hope we are not disturbing you too late in the evening,' said Agatha. 'Remember us?'

'Yes, indeed. Please come in.'

He led them up to his sitting-room on the first floor. It smelt pleasantly of leather from the old leather-bound books which lined the shelves.

'Sherry?' asked William.

'Please,' said Agatha.

He disappeared and came back with a crystal sherry decanter and three glasses. 'Now,' he said, pouring sherry and handing them a glass each, 'how can I help you?'

Agatha quickly outlined the murders of Mrs Witherspoon, Barry Briar and Robin Barley and explained why they were interested in Peter Frampton.

'Now where have I heard that name before? Seventeenth century, you say?'

'Yes, a good-looking man, wavy grey hair, well-tailored, runs a building business.'

'Ah, I think I know whom you mean. Academics can be quite cruel to amateurs. It was, let me see, a few years ago, a colleague at the college invited him to dinner at high table. Unfortunately, Professor Andrew Catsworth – we nickname him Catty – was present.

'Now he considers himself the ultimate authority on the seventeenth century in general and the period of the Civil War in particular. Americans often get confused when we talk about the Civil War, thinking we mean their Civil War in the nineteenth century. Where was I? Ah, yes. Mr Frampton was burning with enthusiasm and seemed to have a good local knowledge. I mean, he had unearthed a lot of local facts from studying old history books of the villages about Worcester. He said he was considering writing a book, a sort of little-known facts of the Commonwealth.'

'Commonwealth?' asked Agatha, wondering if the gentle don had moved on to the twentieth century.

'Cromwell's reign was called the Commonwealth,' explained Charles.

'I knew that,' lied Agatha.

'Then why did you ask?'

'Just showing an intelligent interest,' said Agatha, glaring at Charles.

William cleared his throat apologetically. 'Frampton became quite fired up, saying that the story of a Roundhead officer, John Towdey, had never been published. Evidently the village of Towdey is named after his family who owned the manor-house, long since demolished. This John Towdey fell in love with Sir Geoffrey Lamont's daughter who was staying with friends. Trusting him, she had confided in him that her father had taken refuge with Simon Lovesey. He reported her father's whereabouts to the Cromwellian army. Lamont was taken prisoner and hanged. His daughter, Priscilla, never spoke to Towdey again and it is rumoured she died of a broken heart.

'Professor Catsworth asked in a sneering voice if he had proof of this story. Frampton said it had been handed down through word of mouth. Catsworth proceeded to take Frampton to pieces in front of everyone at the high table. "You amateur historians, always looking for romance, are dangerous," he said. "Concentrate on facts." He began to reel off a list of academic sources proving that it was Lovesey who'd betrayed Lamont. Then he ended up by saying that with Frampton's imagination, he ought to be writing historical bodice rippers. Frampton simply rose from

250

the table and walked out. I have never seen a man so furious.

'We ticked the professor off after he'd left and the professor laughed and said he'd made all those facts up and Frampton was too stupid and amateur to realize it. It was a prime piece of academic spite.'

'What was your impression of Frampton?' asked Agatha.

'I was so sorry for him that I didn't form much of an impression except that I did think at first that he was an extremely vain man. But he did not deserve such treatment.'

'It's hardly enough to kill three people over and I can't see the connection anyway,' said Charles.

They talked some more about the case and then left. 'Another dead end,' said Charles as they drove home.

Agatha grumbled agreement, but as they were heading down the hill into Chipping Norton, she said, 'The diary. I forgot the diary.'

'The one Paul's got on his bookshelves? What about it?'

'Just suppose,' said Agatha slowly, 'that Frampton got hold of some records, or some word-of-mouth evidence that Sir Geoffrey Lamont had written that diary. Suppose he thought it was somewhere in Ivy Cottage and might contain evidence of his daughter's love for a Roundhead, he might be desperate to get his hands on it and publish his findings and send the result to Professor Catsworth.'

'That's mad. I mean, I agree he may have wanted to get his hands on the diary, but to kill to get it! Anyway, let's call on Paul. I mean, didn't you read the diary?'

'Only skipped to the bit about the treasure.'

'We'll look in the diary when we get back and see if there's anything about his daughter. And then what? Go to the police? Can you imagine what Runcorn would make of it?'

'But Bill would listen,' said Agatha. 'I mean, they've never really thought of anyone else but Harry.'

'Okay, let's see if your friend, Paul, is at home.'

Paul had just arrived home before them. He had taken Zena back to her cottage and had been kissing her goodnight, more warmly than a married man should, when Peter Frampton had driven up and got out of his car, his face a mask of rage.

Paul had extracted himself and made his escape.

He listened to what Agatha and Charles had to say. They told him about visiting Frampton at his building works, about the visit to the history don and Agatha wondering if Frampton could be crazy enough to kill to get his hands on that diary.

Paul took it down from the bookshelves. 'It'll take some time to read through it,' he warned. 'It's very closely written.'

'I'll make coffee,' said Agatha. 'You read.'

She went off into the kitchen, once so familiar to her. Paul, like the previous owner, John, had not made any great changes to it. She sighed as she located a jar of instant coffee and began to make three mugs of it.

When she returned to the living-room, Charles was slumped on the sofa, half asleep, and Paul was still reading intently. The soft glow of the reading lamp over his head turned his white hair to gold. He was really very attractive, thought Agatha with a pang. I wish Charles would take himself off.

At last Paul gave an exclamation. 'I've got it,' he said. 'Listen to this. "My dearest and only child Priscilla is causing me Distress. She is Enamoured of one John Towdey, a Cromwellian. I have sent word to her forbidding her to see him, but she is a Stubborn child and with me gone, may Disobey me."'

'I really wonder if that's what he was after,' said Agatha. 'I think I'll go and have a talk with Bill tomorrow.'

'You can't say anything about the diary,'

warned Paul. 'We'd need to say how we found it.'

'I won't, but I must say something to turn Bill's mind in Frampton's direction.'

'Why don't we just confront Frampton? Bluff. Tell him we know it's him.'

'This is one time I think the police should handle it. Do you want to come with us tomorrow?'

Charles rose from the sofa and stretched and yawned. 'I'm tired, Aggie. Let's go to bed.'

Paul's face tightened. 'No,' he said curtly. 'I've got work to do.'

After they had gone, Paul was about to put the diary back on the shelves, but decided to find a hiding place for it. He went through to the kitchen and took down an empty metal canister marked 'Pasta', put the diary in and firmly replaced the lid.

He thought that Agatha's idea of telling Bill was useless. They had no hard evidence. He himself thought that the idea that anyone would commit three murders over an old diary was just too far-fetched. But Frampton might know something. He felt Agatha had cut him out of things, forgetting that it was he himself who had cut himself off. Yes, he would go and see Frampton and have a man-to-man chat. Frampton might be a bit mad with him over kissing Zena, but he could explain that away as well.

Bill interviewed Agatha and Charles at police headquarters the next day. Charles thought gloomily that the more Agatha outlined the reason for her suspicions, the weaker it sounded.

At the end of it all, Bill shook his head. 'There's nothing that would justify us pulling him in for questioning. In order to start asking Robin Barley's neighbours if she had ever been seen with him we would require Runcorn's permission and he's not going to give it. There was too much press interest after the last killing and now Runcorn's got a culprit and got the press off his back.'

'Do you know who Robin Barley left her money to in her will?' asked Agatha. 'There was something in the papers about a daughter.'

'Her daughter, Elizabeth, inherits.'

'Elizabeth who?'

'Barley. She never married.'

'And where does she live?'

'Agatha!' cautioned Bill. 'She could have nothing to do with her mother's death.'

'I was thinking of something else.'

Bill studied Agatha for a long moment. She was an infuriating woman. But he, like Agatha, could not think Harry guilty. And Agatha in the past had had a way of unearthing things by simply blundering about.

'She lives in Mircester, in Abbey Lane. I don't have the number.'

'Thanks, Bill.'

'And what was that all about?' asked Charles as they left.

'She might have some of her mother's photographs.'

'So?'

'Well, Peter Frampton might be in some of them. If there are any photographs of the Wormstone Battle of Worcester, he might be somewhere in the crowd. Or her mother might have told Elizabeth something about him.'

'I'm sure the police studied every bit of paper and photograph that Robin had.'

'But they wouldn't be looking for Peter Frampton. Let's go to Abbey Lane. We can walk from here.'

They made their way towards the abbey and then turned into Abbey Lane, which ran down one side of the massive Norman building. There was a newspaper shop on the corner and they found out that Elizabeth Barley lived at Number Twelve.

Abbey Lane consisted of a row of terraced houses dating from the eighteenth century. Agatha rang the bell of Number Twelve. A faded-looking woman wearing an apron answered the door. She had wispy sandy hair, a long, tired white face, and rough red hands.

'Is Miss Barley at home?' asked Agatha.

'I am Miss Barley,' she said. 'Who are you and what do you want?'

Agatha explained who they were and what they were doing. She had repeated this introduction so many times that she could hear her own voice echoing in her ears.

'Photographs? What kind of photographs?'

'There was a mock Battle of Worcester in Wormstone. We wondered if there were any photos of that.'

'I don't know. She had boxes of photos at the studio. I don't know if the police took them away. I haven't had the heart to go round there. I'll give you the key and you can go and look for yourself. Just to be on the safe side, could I see some identification?'

They handed over their cards and driving licences. She studied them for a moment and then handed them back. 'I'll get you the key. Do you know the address?'

'Yes,' said Agatha.

She left them standing on the doorstep and went indoors. 'I wonder what she does, or if she does anything,' said Agatha.

'Don't even think about asking,' said Charles. 'Just let's get that key.'

Elizabeth came back and handed them the key. 'If I'm not here when you return,' she said, 'just put it through the letter-box.'

They thanked her and walked off, Agatha

setting a brisk pace, frightened Elizabeth would change her mind and call them back.

'If the studio is still sealed by the police, we can't break in, Aggie.'

'She wasn't murdered there. Hurry up, Charles.'

There was no police seal or tape outside Robin's studio. They let themselves in.

There were canvases stacked against the wall and a covered painting on an easel. There was none of the usual messy clutter of the artist. Paints and brushes were ranged in order on a clean bench. They began to search. There were two chairs and a sofa where Agatha had once sat talking to Robin in one section of the studio with a coffee table. The kitchen had a round table and two chairs. Off the other end of the studio was a small bedroom with a large wardrobe. Agatha opened the wardrobe. There were only a few clothes hanging there. Obviously Robin had kept most of her personal belongings in Wormstone. But at the bottom of the wardrobe were two large cardboard boxes.

Agatha opened one and found it full of photographs. 'Bingo!' she said. 'I'll take one and you take the other.'

They carried the boxes into the studio and began to search. At one point Charles got up and examined the canvases against the wall. He sat down again. 'She painted from photographs, Aggie. My box is full of photographs of the Cotswolds. I don't think we're going to find any personal photographs here. We should have asked for the key to the house in Wormstone.'

'Keep searching,' said Agatha doggedly. 'There might be something. Ah, down at the bottom of this box are photographs of people, portrait photographs. She must have painted portraits from the photographs.'

'Recognize anyone?'

'Not yet.'

They worked on until Charles said with a sigh, 'No Battle of Worcester. No Peter Frampton. Let's go back and see if the obliging Elizabeth can let us get into the house in Wormstone. I'll put the boxes back where we found them.'

Agatha, who had been sitting on the sofa, stood up. She felt flat. Her eyes fell on the canvases. Had Robin been a good painter? She began to turn some around. They were indeed paintings of the Cotswolds, drawn precisely from photographs, competent and lifeless. She turned round some more and came across the portrait of a woman.

'What are you doing?' asked Charles.

'Looking for a portrait of Peter Frampton.'

'Oh, Aggie, I'm getting a bad feeling about this. The man's probably innocent.'

Agatha ignored him and continued to search the paintings. 'Well, well,' she said. 'Come and look at this.'

She heaved a large canvas out and turned it around so that Charles could see it. It was a portrait of Peter Frampton wearing nothing but a hard hat. It was not very well executed but none-theless the subject was clearly Peter Frampton.

'Got him!' said Agatha triumphantly.

'So what do we do now? Go and confront him?'

'Not on your life. I decided never to confront murderers again. Too dangerous. We'll tell Bill about it and let the police take it from there.'

Paul was puzzled. He had confronted Peter Frampton at the building works about the diary. Peter had simply laughed and said he must be mad if he thought anyone would murder three people over a diary. Paul had tried to get him to betray himself by saying that he had the diary. But Frampton showed no reaction. He was so much at ease and so friendly that Paul began to feel ridiculous.

'Anyway, now you're here,' said Peter, 'come and I'll give you the royal tour.'

'I really should be getting back.'

'Oh, come on. I'm proud of the place. Where is this mysterious diary, by the way?'

'At my cottage in Carsely.'

'How did you get it?'

'Bit of detective work,' said Paul vaguely.

'Ah, you amateur detectives.' He led Paul through metal sheds piled high with bricks, sheds full of sacks of concrete, and other – what Paul privately termed – dreadfully boring machinery.

'I really should be going,' said Paul. 'Thank you for your time.'

'There's just one other place you should see. It's where I keep all the history books in storage that I haven't room for at home. You'll be amazed at the amount I've got.'

Might as well see it, thought Paul. Might just be something there.

Frampton strode ahead. They were reaching the end of the development and Paul could not see any building in sight. The main buildings seemed a long way behind them.

Frampton came to a stop. 'Down here.'

'Down where?' asked Paul.

Frampton laughed. 'Can't see anything yet, can you? It's an old Anderson shelter left over from World War Two.'

He pointed, and now stepping forward, Paul could see steps leading down underground. The shelter on the surface was totally covered in grass and weeds.

'Damn, I've something in my shoe. Go on down and I'll join you.'

Paul went down the steps and pushed open the door. It was pitch-black inside. He groped forward, feeling for a light switch. The door behind him slammed shut. He whipped round and flung himself at the door just as he heard a bar being lowered on the outside.

'Stay here until you come to your senses.' Frampton's voice came faintly through the door. 'I'll come every day. If you tell me where that

261

diary is, I'll let you out. Twenty-four hours in here and you'll feel like talking.'

Paul hammered on the door and shouted until he was exhausted. Then he groped his way around his 'prison' until his hands felt the outline of a candle. He remembered he had picked up a book of matches in the French restaurant. He was wearing his best suit, the one he had worn the night before. He fished out the matches and struck one and lit the candle. There was a bench running along the earthen walls. He was too young to remember Anderson shelters, but he suddenly remembered hearing about them in a documentary about the war. There must have been houses here at one time. They were usually built at the bottom of gardens, the idea of the underground shelters being that they could not be seen from the air. He slumped down on the bench. He would have to tell Frampton where the diary was. He would go mad if he was locked in here for days.

Bill and two policemen called at the building works in the late afternoon, to be told that Mr Frampton had gone home. But when they called at his house, there was no answer.

'Paul still isn't home,' fretted Agatha. 'Do you think we should go along to his cottage and get the diary?'

'We can't break in.'

'I've still got a key. The lock hasn't been changed since James lived there.'

'Okay,' said Charles. 'It's better than sitting here doing nothing.'

They walked along and went into Paul's cottage.

'His MG isn't outside,' said Agatha.

Inside the cottage, Charles went straight to the bookshelves. 'It's not here!' he said. 'Maybe the silly bugger took it somewhere.'

'I don't think he would. Look around.'

They searched carefully through the books and behind the books. Then they went through the drawers in his desk. 'I'll try upstairs,' said Charles. 'You look in the kitchen.'

'Why the kitchen?'

'People always seem to think the kitchen's a safe hiding place. I had a great-aunt who kept a diamond necklace inside a bag of frozen peas.'

Agatha discounted the freezer and the fridge. Surely Paul would not be stupid enough to hide a valuable diary there. She checked behind the cans and boxes of groceries, in the rubbish bin, and behind the plates on the dresser. She remembered taking plates off this very dresser and smashing them on the floor in a rage in one of her fights with James. She sat down at the table, suddenly torn with memories. Would she ever see James again? Her eyes blurred with tears and she wiped them angrily away. She found herself looking at a neat row of canisters on the counter of the dresser – sugar, coffee, flour and pasta.

She got to her feet and began to prise open the lids. In the pasta one, she found the diary.

Agatha went to the foot of the stairs and called, 'Found it!'

Charles came pattering lightly down the stairs. 'Good, let's keep it until Paul comes back.'

'If the police ever find we've got it, we'll be in real trouble,' said Agatha.

They walked to Agatha's cottage. The village was quiet and peaceful. This is the last case, thought Agatha. To throw away peace and quiet for all this business – it's ridiculous.

'What are you thinking?' asked Charles as they walked through to the kitchen and petted the cats.

'I've just been thinking that I could have such a pleasant quiet life in this village if I left it all to the police in future,' said Agatha.

'You'd go mad with boredom. Ever think of moving back to London?'

'I don't fit in there any more. It doesn't seem the same.'

'Ever think of opening a detective agency?'

'I've been asked that before. It would involve missing cats and messy divorces.'

'Still, it might be better than just sitting here.'

'I wouldn't just sit here,' protested Agatha. 'I'd become like Mrs Bloxby and involve myself in good works.'

'You're not Mrs Bloxby and never could be.'

'Oh, she's a saint and I could never rise to her heights?'

'Don't quarrel, Aggie. Let's go out for dinner. Bill will contact us if he's got anything.'

They enjoyed a pleasant dinner. I'm glad Charles is back in my life, thought Agatha. I was silly about Paul. But Charles would not stay for long. He never did. She often wondered what he really thought of her.

When they returned to her cottage, she phoned Paul but there was no reply. She locked up for the night and they both went to their respective beds. The night was humid and warm. Agatha tossed and turned, suddenly uneasy about Paul. Where had he gone?

She groaned and got up. She would just look out of her front door and see if his car was outside. The old banger he had bought had been there earlier but the MG had been missing.

Agatha unbolted and unlocked the front door after switching off the burglar alarm. She glanced at her watch. One in the morning. Paul's MG was outside his cottage. Good. He was safe and sound.

She was about to close the door when she stiffened. Something was not quite right. She opened the door wide and walked out on to the step and looked along. Suddenly she saw a flickering light at one of the downstairs windows. It was like the light from a pencil torch. Paul would hardly be looking around his own cottage with a torch.

Agatha closed the door quietly and ran upstairs and woke Charles. 'What is it?' he grumbled. 'I've only just dropped off. Too hot in this cottage. Why don't you get air-conditioning?'

'Listen. Paul's MG is parked outside his cottage but someone's in there with a torch. It can't be Paul.'

Charles got up and dressed hurriedly. 'You wait here and I'll creep along and have a look.'

Agatha went to her own room and got dressed. Maybe Paul had had some sort of power cut. She went downstairs to meet Charles, who was coming back. 'There's a full moon,' he said. 'I knelt down and peered in the front window. It's Frampton!'

'Oh, my God. What has he done with Paul?'

'Phone Bill,' said Charles. 'If he's killed three people, he won't hesitate to kill us.'

Agatha phoned Bill's home. He answered the phone himself and she was grateful she did not have to explain anything to his mother.

She told him about Frampton being in Paul's cottage.

'Sit tight,' ordered Bill. 'We'll be along as fast as possible.'

After she had rung off, Charles said, 'Let's have a drink. All we have to do is wait. Even if he's gone by the time the police arrive, he'll need to explain why he was driving Paul's car and what he was doing in the cottage.'

Agatha shuddered. 'He may not have been

266

driving Paul's car. He may have forced Paul to drive it.'

Charles poured drinks and they sat uneasily, waiting. Half an hour passed.

'Did you lock the front door?' asked Charles.

'I was so upset I forgot,' said Agatha. 'I'll do it now.'

She was just getting to her feet when the sitting-room door opened and Peter Frampton walked in, a small pistol in his hand. 'The diary,' he snarled. 'Where is it?'

'What diary?' asked Charles.

'Don't waste my time.' Frampton's pupils were like pin-points. Agatha was sure he was on some sort of drug.

'You can't shoot us,' said Agatha. 'You've already murdered three people. I mean, why go to such elaborate lengths when you could just have shot them?' She thought she heard a movement outside. Bill?

'The first,' said Frampton calmly, 'was supposed to look like an accident. I knew about that secret passage. I thought I could frighten the old bitch out of there, but she wouldn't move. Then dear Robin came on the phone. I'd had an affair with her. She knew nothing, but she was hinting that she would tell the police about what she called my obsession with finding that diary. So she had to go. And just when I thought I was in the clear, that idiot, Briar, started to blackmail me. He'd been out in the fields with his dog during the night I was at Ivy Cottage and he said he had seen me leaving. Diary, and quick about it.'

'I don't know what diary you're talking about,' said Agatha loudly.

'Sir Geoffrey Lamont's diary. I read in an old manuscript that he had told one of his fellow prisoners before his death that it was hidden in Ivy Cottage. If I had that, I'd publish my findings and make my mark on the historical scene. I need it. Get it. I'll show that dried-up old stick of a professor. No one humiliates me! I'll start off by shooting you in the kneecaps and I'll keep on shooting until one of you cracks.'

The door crashed open. Bill stood there, flanked by two armed policemen. 'Drop your weapon and lie on the floor,' he ordered.

Frampton looked down at the gun in his hand. Then, quick as a flash, he raised it and shot himself through the head.

Agatha stood white and shaking as his body slumped to the floor.

Charles put an arm around Agatha and led her from the room and Bill took out his mobile phone and dialled and began to rap out instructions.

They waited in the kitchen. The forensic team arrived, Runcorn and Evans arrived and the police pathologist arrived.

At last Runcorn, flanked by Evans, joined them in the kitchen. They made statements about how they had seen someone shining a torch in Paul's cottage, how Charles had gone along and recognized Frampton and how they had phoned Bill.

Runcorn eyed them narrowly. 'DC Wong heard Frampton confess to the three murders. It seemed he wanted to get his hands on some old diary. He thought you'd got it. Have you got it?'

'No,' lied Agatha. If she admitted they had it, she could be charged with obstructing the police in an investigation and then she would have to tell them where she'd found it.

'Sir Charles?'

'Haven't a clue what he was babbling on about,' said Charles.

'Then you don't mind if we search this cottage? I can always get a warrant.'

Charles felt a stab of alarm. He didn't know where Agatha had hidden it.

'Go ahead,' said Agatha. 'But we've got to find Paul.'

'You'll stay right where you are until we've searched the place.'

Charles and Agatha sat huddled together at the kitchen table. 'Where did you hide it?' whispered Charles.

'Where he'll never find it.'

'Aggie, they'll even look in the flowerpots.'

'Shh. Here's Bill.'

Bill sat down next to them. 'We've got our murderer, thanks to you, Agatha. But what's all this about a diary? And what put you on to Frampton?'

'Woman's intuition. I never liked him,' said Agatha. 'It was when we searched Robin's studio and found that portrait we knew he had lied about never having met her.'

'They'll be in here shortly to search the kitchen for that diary he was talking about.'

'The man was mad,' said Agatha. 'Obsessed over some old diary. We went to see a history don in Oxford.' She told him how Frampton had been humiliated by the professor.

'And you're sure you don't have that diary?'

'Absolutely not.'

'If you say so. Of course, it wouldn't surprise me if you and Paul had found that secret passage and somehow found this diary.'

The police entered the kitchen to start their search.

Agatha felt a wave of delayed shock. She said, 'I'm going up to bed. You know where I am.'

Charles followed her upstairs. On the landing, he said, 'Where did –' but was silenced by Agatha putting a hand over his lips.

'Go to bed, Charles,' she said.

Fully dressed, Agatha huddled under the duvet, shivering despite the warmth of the night. She fell asleep and was wakened two hours later by Bill shaking her shoulder.

'They haven't found anything,' he said. 'You must have hidden it well.'

'I don't know what you're talking about,' said Agatha, struggling up.

'You're both to report to police headquarters in the morning and we'll go over your statements.'

'Okay. Just go away,' moaned Agatha.

But after Bill had gone, she lay awake, listening until she heard them all drive off. She went downstairs, her face tightening in anger when she saw the mess in the kitchen. Even a bag of flour had been slit open. The fact that the bag had been lying on the shelves for two years waiting for her to blossom into a baker did nothing to appease her anger.

She swung round as Charles entered the kitchen. 'What a wreck!' he exclaimed. 'Where's the diary?'

'Come upstairs and I'll show you.'

Agatha went into her bedroom and over to an antique travelling case on her dressing-table which she used to keep her bits of jewellery and the few letters she had once received from James. 'It's got a secret drawer,' she said. 'I bought this on a whim in that antiques market in Oxford, the one that's now closed down.' She fumbled at the back. 'See!' She turned the case around. A drawer had sprung open at the back and inside lay the diary.

'What are we going to do with it?'

Agatha closed the drawer. 'I don't know about you, but I need more sleep and then I'll think of something.' She suddenly put her hands up to her face. 'Charles! We've forgotten about Paul. What's happened to him?'

Chapter Eleven

Paul sat in the darkness of the Anderson shelter. He had tried shouting and screaming but it had only left him feeling helpless and exhausted. He thought of his wife, Juanita. Why on earth had he been so stubborn about staying in the Cotswolds? Why hadn't he gone to Madrid? It was all Agatha's fault – silly blundering woman.

He wondered whether he should try praying. He didn't believe in God. Never had. Still, he had once heard someone say there are no agnostics on the battlefield. He would give it a try. He sank to his knees on the earthen floor and prayed desperately for deliverance.

As he rose from his knees, he heard police sirens faintly in the distance and was overcome with religious awe. Juanita was a devout Catholic. He would no longer mock her faith. They would go to church together, start a family, live a decent married life. He waited and waited. Then he flung himself at the door and shouted and screamed.

Nobody came.

* * *

Agatha phoned Bill at police headquarters and listened in fear as he said that they had been out to the building works and combed the place from end to end, they had turned over Frampton's cottage, but no sign of Paul. Zena and workers at the building works remembered seeing Paul, but no one had seen him leave. Agatha rang off and told Charles what he had said.

'Let's go over there,' said Charles. 'We might find out something they haven't.'

But when they got to the building works it was to find out the place had been closed down after the police left. A solitary watchman told them that the workers had decided to go home until they found out whether some executor of Frampton's estate was going to pay their wages.

Agatha said they wanted to search the buildings. He was about to refuse until Agatha crackled a fifty-pound note in front of his eyes. So through the buildings they went, hoping to see something that the police had missed, but it seemed hopeless.

The day was very hot and sunny. A heat haze shimmered across the fields beside the works. They thanked the watchman and then stood wondering what to do.

'If he wanted to get rid of Paul,' said Agatha, 'he wouldn't surely do it anywhere there was a chance of being seen. Let's walk round the perimeter fence – like over there.'

'But there's nothing over there, Aggie, except grass and weeds.'

'Come on. There might be a dead body in the grass.'

'Bang, bang! You're dead!' shrilled a voice and Agatha clutched her heart. A small child rose out of the long grass, followed by another. Both were wearing miniature Stetsons and carrying toy guns.

'Beat it!' snarled Agatha.

The children looked up at her, not in the least afraid. They were both white-faced and spotty and had calculating eyes. Why do people insist that kids are innocent? wondered Agatha.

'Got any sweets?' asked one.

'Get lost.'

'If you give us sweets, we'll show you where the ghost lives.'

Agatha was just wondering whether to bang their heads together when Charles said, 'What ghost?'

'No sweets, no tell,' they chorused.

Charles held out a pound coin. 'Tell us.'

They looked at each other and solemnly shook their heads. 'Not enough,' said the spottier of the two.

'Oh, here!' said Agatha impatiently, handing over a five-pound note. Anything that might lead them to Paul was worth any money.

'Okay, follow us.'

They followed the children to where a taller mound of grass lay by the perimeter fence. 'It lives in there,' said the spotty one. 'Moaning and yelling.'

Agatha walked round the mound and saw the stairs leading down. 'It's an old war shelter,' she called excitedly. Followed by Charles, she went down the steps and then, with his help, lifted the heavy metal bar which guarded the door.

The door swung open and sunlight flooded in, illuminating Paul, who was lying in the foetal position on the floor.

'Paul!' cried Agatha. 'Thank God we've found you!'

Paul had been crying with fear and despair. He rose to his feet, furious at his weakness, and turned all his venom on Agatha.

'Just keep away from me, you horrible old bat!' he shouted. 'If you hadn't got me involved in your stupid detective work, this would never have happened.'

Agatha turned away in disgust. Then she turned back. 'Sit down, you useless twat. Just shut up. You're going nowhere until the police and ambulance come.'

She pulled out her mobile phone and asked urgently for police and ambulance. Then she walked outside and lit a cigarette. Charles stayed behind and looked down at Paul, who was sitting on the bench, his head bowed.

'The police were here earlier,' said Charles mildly. 'Searched the place end to end. If it hadn't been for Aggie and me, you'd have rotted here.'

'Where's Frampton?' croaked Paul.

'Dead. Shot himself after he threatened me and Aggie with a gun. Shot himself when the police arrived.'

'Have you any water?'

'No, but the ambulance will be here soon enough.'

Charles went outside to join Agatha. 'Don't take it too hard,' he said. 'The man's in shock.'

Agatha shrugged and puffed energetically on her cigarette. Why did things never work out the way she imagined them? She had dreamt on the road to the building works that she would find Paul and he would be so grateful he would take her in his arms and propose marriage. It was only when they began to search the works that she feared he was dead. Why on earth would a murderer like Frampton leave him alive? To find the diary, of course.

Agatha whipped round and went down into the shelter. 'Look here,' she said, 'for God's sake don't mention that bloody diary or we'll be in the soup.'

'Okay,' muttered Paul, looking at the floor.

'The story's this. Charles and I found a portrait of Frampton in Robin's studio. We phoned you and you came here to question Frampton, who locked you up until he figured out what to do with you.'

'All right!' shouted Paul.

'They're coming,' said Charles from outside. 'I'll run and meet them and guide them here.'

When Paul had been taken off to hospital for a check, Agatha and Charles found themselves facing an angry Runcorn. 'You two,' he said, 'were supposed to report to police headquarters today to go over your statements.'

'Well, we couldn't,' said Agatha. 'Because we were doing your work for you. If it hadn't been for us, you'd have had another body on your hands.'

'You are to go to Mircester now. DC Wong will accompany you and take your statements.'

At that moment Bill came up. 'Good work,' he said and earned himself a furious glare from his superior officer.

At police headquarters, Agatha and Charles added their experience of finding Paul to their statements. Agatha was aware the whole time of Bill's intelligent eyes on her face as she talked so that she could almost see a picture of the diary rising above her head as if on a film.

At last Bill switched off the tape and told them to wait until their statements were typed up.

'Don't be too hard on Paul,' said Charles. 'It must have been hell being shut in there.'

'He called me old,' muttered Agatha. 'I'll never forgive him.'

'Oh, come on.'

'To forgive is divine, Charles, and I ain't divine. I want to get home and sleep for a week. I phoned Doris Simpson before we left and she said she would have the place all cleaned up. I'll pay her well.'

'But you already pay her for the cleaning. Why pay more?'

'Because, Scrooge, the mess the place was in is above and beyond the call of duty.'

'I think we should call on Mrs Bloxby when we get out of here.'

'Why?'

'Because she's a friend. She'll be worried about you.'

It seemed to take ages to get the statements signed and it was two hours later before Agatha and Charles sat in the vicarage garden telling Mrs Bloxby about their adventures.

'What will you do with the diary?' asked Mrs Bloxby when they had finished.

'I just thought of a way out,' said Agatha. 'We'll take it to William Dalrymple, that history don in Oxford, the one I met on another case. We'll tell him all and see if he'll help us by claiming he discovered it in a box in the college library or something. I'll be glad to be rid of it. Where's your lesser half?'

'He's gone to see the bishop.'

'No trouble, I hope?'

'No, it's good news. The bishop has received money from the Lotteries Commission for the restoration of old churches. We're to get some for the church roof. Which reminds me. One of the parishioners gave Alf a present of trout. Do stay to dinner.'

And Charles, aware of the horrors of Agatha's deep freeze, quickly accepted.

Later, as they walked to Agatha's cottage, she said, 'I wonder if the press will be waiting on the doorstep.'

'Doubt it,' said Charles. 'Runcorn will make sure the police get all the credit and you get none.'

'The press'll all be outside Mircester police headquarters,' said Agatha wistfully. 'It'd be nice to go there and put them straight.'

'Leave it, Aggie. We're too tired.'

Agatha's cottage was clean once more. She played with the cats and then went up to have a bath and go to bed. She put on the black see-through nightie because it was cool, but she could not help feeling silly when she thought she had bought it for Paul's benefit.

She was just getting into bed when the doorbell rang. Agatha went through to Charles's room but he was fast asleep.

She sighed and went downstairs. Suddenly aware that she had nothing on but the black

279

nightie, she opened the door a crack and peered round it.

Paul Chatterton stood there holding a large bouquet of flowers. 'I'm so sorry,' he said. 'I owe you my life. Agatha, please forgive me.'

Overcome by gladness, Agatha seized a wrap from the hallstand and put it round her and then opened the door wide. 'What beautiful flowers!' she said.

Paul smiled. 'For a beautiful woman.' He bent to kiss her. And that was when Juanita leapt on his back, screaming and cursing in Spanish. Agatha tried to retreat and close the door on them but Juanita suddenly jumped down from Paul's back, squeezed in front of him, and shouted, 'You whore.' She whipped off Agatha's wrap and glared at her nightie. Then she grabbed the flowers and jumped up and down on them.

'Anything the matter, darling?' asked Charles from behind Agatha. He moved her aside and glared at Juanita. 'Why are you shouting at my fiancée?'

She goggled at him. 'Your . . .?'

'Yes,' said Charles firmly. 'Today she saved your husband's life and this is all the thanks she gets.' He pulled Agatha back and shut the door on Paul and his wife.

'Thanks,' said Agatha weakly.

'Any time,' said Charles cheerfully. 'That nightie is very revealing. Feel like a bit of nookie?'

'No,' said Agatha crossly and stumped off up the stairs.

A month later Agatha answered the door to Bill Wong. 'No Charles?' he asked.

'No, he's long gone,' said Agatha. 'Paul, too. Paul's moved to Spain and he's going to rent out his cottage.'

'I'm sorry I haven't been round earlier. Something strange has happened.'

'Oh, what?'

'Do you know an Oxford don called William Dalrymple?'

'Can't recall if I do.'

'Agatha! One of the reasons you were interested in Frampton was because, as you told me, you visited some history don in Oxford.'

'Oh, yes, *that* William Dalrymple.'

'He claims to have bought a box of books at an auction and he found Sir Geoffrey Lamont's diary.'

'My heavens! What a coincidence!'

'Indeed. Particularly as you knew him. Look, Agatha, the case is closed, thanks to you. But here's what I think. I think you and Paul found it when you were investigating that secret passage and had to find a way of getting rid of it.'

'What a fertile imagination you do have.'

'Not nearly as fertile as yours. I assume Harry and Carol came to thank you.'

'Yes, they did.'

281

'And did they pay you anything?'

'Well, no. But I didn't ask.'

'Agatha, if you ever get involved in murder again – and I hope you don't – you should try earning some money.'

'I'll think about it.'

'We've been digging into Frampton's background. He was once a mining engineer in South Africa. That explains the cyanide pellets. And there's something else. While he was living in Durban, he was dating a young girl who subsequently disappeared. She was never found. The police in Durban are reopening that case. We found a quantity of cocaine in his cottage, hidden under the floor-boards, together with *his* diary. He was passionate about making his mark in the world with some great academic historical find.'

'Funny how some people can go quite mad without anyone around them realizing it,' said Agatha. 'I'm glad it's over.'

'By the way, it was Briar who slit the roof of Paul's MG and threw the CD player in the ditch.'

'How on earth did you find that out?'

'Some crusty old codger from Hebberdon came forward with the information. All he would say was that Briar didn't like the looks of the pair of you and wanted to frighten you off from coming back.'

'Why didn't he talk about this before?'

'I think they were all a bit frightened of Briar.'

They talked some more and to Agatha's relief, Bill did not mention the diary again.

After he had left, she thought about Harry and Carol taking her services for free.

The phone rang. It was Roy Silver. Agatha bragged away happily about her brilliance in solving the case. Roy listened patiently and then said, 'I've got a PR job that might interest you.'

Agatha took a deep breath. 'I'm out of PR. Not going to do any again.'

'Why?'

Agatha grinned.

'Because I'm going to start my own detective agency.'

Agatha Raisin and the Deadly Dance

Agatha waltzes into yet another murder investigation!

Can the feisty Agatha cut it as a private investigator? She soon learns that running her own detective agency in the Cotswolds is not quite like starring in a Raymond Chandler movie. But then in walks wealthy divorcee Catherine Laggat-Brown, and Agatha is given her first real case.

Death threats, blackmail and worse soon follow, and once again Agatha is off scouring the countryside for clues and showing friends and enemies alike what Raisin Investigations can do!

Praise for M.C. Beaton and the Agatha Raisin series

'Compare this one to lemon meringue pie: light . . . with a delicious hint of tartness at its heart.'   *Washington Times*

'Beaton's dry sense of humour and her unflattering but affectionate portrait of gruff, often adolescent-acting Agatha makes this . . . a bloom worth plucking'   *Publishers Weekly*

£5.99

Agatha Raisin
and the Perfect Paragon

After almost meeting a sticky end thanks to a hired hit man and her former secretary, Agatha could use some low-key cases. So when Robert Smedley walks through the door of her detective agency, determined to prove his wife is cheating on him, Agatha immediately offers her help.

Mabel Smedley seems to be the perfect wife: young, pretty, and a regular volunteer at church. But just as Agatha is ready to give up, Robert Smedley is poisoned with weed killer leaving Mabel to inherit a fortune. With no one left to pay her, Agatha is forced to drop the investigation . . . that is, until her old friend Sir Charles Fraith rekindles her curiosity.

Praise for M.C. Beaton and
the Agatha Raisin series

'M. C. Beaton has created a national treasure.'
Anne Robinson

'The Miss Marple-like Raisin is a refreshingly sensible, wonderfully eccentric, thoroughly likeable heroine.'   *Booklist*

£5.99

Agatha Raisin
and Love, Lies and Liquor

Sand, sea – and a cell for Agatha!

Agatha Raisin thinks she's in for a treat when her ex-husband, James Lacey, invites her on a holiday with him. But horror! His idea of an idyllic break is the small, run-down resort of Snoth-on-Sea. And from there on, naturally things go from bad to worse. When a fellow guest in their hotel is found murdered, Agatha herself becomes a suspect – she must solve this particular case from a prison cell!

Praise for M.C. Beaton and
the Agatha Raisin series

'Beaton has a winner in the irrepressible, romance-hungry Agatha.'   *Chicago Sun-Times*

'Clever red herrings and some wicked unfinished business guarantees that the listener will pant for a sequel'   *The Times*, audio review

£17.99

A Load of Old Bones

by Suzette Hill

Dire doings at the vicarage!

A Load of Old Bones takes a nostalgic romp through 1950s mythical Surrey, where murky deeds and shady characters abound! All that Reverend Francis Oughterard had ever wanted was an easy life and a bit of peace and quiet. Instead, he gets entangled in a nightmare world of accidental murder, predatory female parishioners, officious policemen, oddball clerics, wrathful old ladies and a drunken bishop. As the vicar's life spirals out of control it is up to his supercilious cat and bone-obsessed hound to help save his skin . . .

Praise for *A Load of Old Bones*

'I think this is tremendous – amusing and professional'   Dame Beryl Bainbridge

'An enchanting tale, beautifully written, full of fun, wit and insight'
The very Reverend Alex Witherspoon,
Dean Emeritus of Guildford

Publication June 2007
£18.99

No. of copies	Order	Title	RRP	Total
		Agatha Raisin and the Quiche of Death	£5.99	
		Agatha Raisin and the Vicious Vet	£5.99	
		Agatha Raisin and the Potted Gardener	£5.99	
		Agatha Raisin and the Walkers of Dembley	£5.99	
		Agatha Raisin and the Murderous Marriage	£5.99	
		Agatha Raisin and the Terrible Tourist	£5.99	
		Agatha Raisin and the Wellspring of Death	£5.99	
		Agatha Raisin and the Wizard of Evesham	£5.99	
		Agatha Raisin and the Witch of Wyckhadden	£5.99	
		Agatha Raisin and the Fairies of Fryfam	£5.99	
		Agatha Raisin and the Love from Hell	£5.99	
		Agatha Raisin and the Day the Floods Came	£5.99	
		Agatha Raisin and the Curious Curate	£5.99	
		Agatha Raisin and the Deadly Dance	£5.99	
		Agatha Raisin and the Perfect Paragon	£5.99	
		Agatha Raisin and Love, Lies and Liquor	£17.99	
		Grand Total		£

Please feel free to order any other titles that do not appear on this order form!

Name: _____

Address: _____

_____ Postcode: _____

Daytime Tel. No./Email: _____
(in case of query)

Three ways to pay:

1. *For express service telephone the TBS order line on 01206 255 800 and quote 'AR'. Order lines are open Monday–Friday, 8:30am–5:30pm*

2. I enclose a cheque made payable to **TBS Ltd** for £ _____

3. Please charge my ☐ Visa ☐ Mastercard ☐ Amex ☐ Switch

(Switch issue no. _____)

Card number: _____

Expiry date: _____ Signature: _____
(your signature is essential when paying by credit card)

Please return forms (*no stamp required*) to, FREEPOST RLUL-SJGC-SGKJ, Cash Sales/Direct Mail Dept, The Book Service, Colchester Road, Frating, Colchester CO7 7DW.

Enquiries to: readers@constablerobinson.com
www.constablerobinson.com

Constable and Robinson Ltd (directly or via its agents) may email or phone you about promotions or products.
☐ Tick box if you do not want these from us ☐ or our subsidiaries